# AN UNEXPECTED SEQUEL

## PARANORMAL TALENT AGENCY

### EPISODE FOUR

HEATHER SILVIO

Panther Books

Published in the United States by Panther Books, Las Vegas.

Correspondence to the author may be sent to:
heather@heathersilvio.com

Cover design by Sonia Freitas at Chloe Belle Arts
https://ChloeBelleArts.com



ISBN (Print) 978-1-7326938-5-2
ISBN (E-book) 978-1-7326938-6-9

# BOOKS BY HEATHER SILVIO

## PARANORMAL TALENT AGENCY

Lights, Camera, Action (Episode One)

Reset to One (Episode Two)

That's a Wrap (Episode Three)

An Unexpected Sequel (Episode Four)

Jumping the Shark (Episode Five)

The Season Finale (Episode Six)

## NON-SERIES FICTION

Not Quite Famous: A Romantic Comedy of an Actress
on the Edge

Beyond the Abyss: Tales of the Supernatural

Courting Death

## NONFICTION

Special Snowflake Syndrome: The Unrecognized
Personality Disorder Destroying the World

Happiness by the Numbers: 9 Steps to Authentic
Happiness

Stress Disorders: A Healing Path for PTSD

# ACKNOWLEDGMENTS

Thank you to my mentor who helped me hone the continuing
story of the Paranormal Talent Agency.

# CHAPTER ONE

As the founder and owner of Landon Talent Agency, could I ever have predicted I'd make a deal with the devil? Okay, technically, Barbara Knollman was a low-level demon. But still. I'd agreed to do the demon's bidding and, if I wasn't yet entirely sorry for having made that deal, I definitely had regrets.

Now I sat in the overstuffed leather chair opposite the Councilwoman, my hands clasped in my lap, eyes downcast like I'd been called to the principal's office. Though, in a way, that was true.

"Robin, this has worked out perfectly," Barbara said. She stood at the window overlooking Main Street, immobile, her brown hair swept back in a tight bun. She returned to her chair behind the imposing solid wood desk and sat, her hands resting on its surface, talon-like fingernails displayed.

The effect worked. I swallowed audibly and Barbara chuckled. "You really wanted the supernatural underworld to be exposed?" I asked. A few months ago, a local pain-in-the-butt reporter revealed a crazy genie to be a serial killer. And then outed the lot of us.

Barbara smiled, her small sharp teeth drawing attention. "Yes. I did. I foresaw the path to my success. It included the exposure," she explained, tapping her manicured talons against the fine wood-grain.

"I'm not sure I understand what this has been about," I admitted in a small voice. My boss could see the future, but she kept her visions a secret. Even I didn't know what success she sought.

Barbara looked down on me, her minion. "You will. Everyone will." A demon posing as a 50-something year-old human, she also happened to be the unofficial head of the Las Vegas City Council. Technically that position fell to the Mayor, but Barbara held the actual power. Interestingly, although the paranormal underworld had been exposed, she had not. I wondered if she saw that in her vision.

My skin crawled as she stared at me, an ambiguous smile on her face. Now what? I waited. It would do no good to ask. After five years as her minion, I certainly learned my place. Maybe I used to be a witch, but today I was powerless and under her thumb.

"It's time for the next step," the Councilwoman stated. "You will shut down your agency."

I gasped. Shut down my agency?

"I want your full focus and attention. There is a being in town who must be eliminated."

Surely she doesn't mean—

"And you will eliminate him."

My jaw dropped open and I stared, aghast, at the demon. Close my agency and kill someone? I needed to buy time. "Who?"

"His name is Jackson McKee."

I waited to see if more information would be forthcoming. Nada. I risked her wrath. "Who is Jackson McKee?"

She gave me a withering look. "It doesn't matter. I need him killed."

I blanched at her tone and directive – and pushed back. "If I don't know what kind of paranormal being he is," I reasoned, "how will I know how to kill him?"

Barbara pursed her lips. "He's human, but with abilities."

Hmm. A witch like me? An empath like Catherine, that irritating fellow talent agent?

"So you can kill him like any other human."

I paled but nodded. Where was she going with this? "Okay. Where do I find him?"

"He's about to be a cameraman on *Forbidden Island.*"

I remembered receiving character breakdowns for actor submissions for that film and seized my opening. "Since it's a movie production, maybe it would make sense to keep my agency open so I have a natural in to get on set. After all, I sent actors to it."

Barbara stared impassively. I wasn't stupid. I knew she knew why I made my suggestion. She sighed. "Fine. Keep your agency open. I want him dead within the week."

I gulped.

She glanced down at the paperwork on her desk. I took that as my cue to leave and scurried out of her office, with nary a backward glance. I wasn't a killer. What could I do now?

# CHAPTER TWO

The drive back to my office passed in a blur. I remained on autopilot while I considered my options. I was a glorified gopher for Barbara. That was it. She'd never asked me to kill someone before. Why would she ask me now? Could she have seen it in a vision? Surely not.

I zipped my black VW Jetta coupe into my designated spot outside the office building housing Landon Talent Agency but remained seated for a few minutes, my mind still buzzing. It wouldn't hurt to do a little digging, at least find out who this Jackson McKee was. Maybe he deserved to die.

The wind whipped against me when I exited the vehicle. I shuddered and pulled my beige coat tighter. Even in Vegas, December could be uncomfortably cold.

Who was I kidding?

I wasn't going to kill this guy.

I hurried into the two-story stucco building, took the stairs up to my locked office. I maintained a small enough agency that I didn't need to keep regular business hours or employ an assistant. I barely noticed the gray couches and end table with a lamp on it as I moved through the space. The office had come furnished. The furnishings did the job. I closed the door to my inner sanctum behind me and collapsed into my rolling chair, the one piece of furniture I had paid for. My butt needed to be comfortable!

My laptop quietly booted up, and I found my eye drawn to the only personal touch I'd added to my office. A picture of my childhood cat, Patches, his scraggly image in the frame I'd designed. The black, white, and orange stray had shown up one day and stayed with me for years, vanishing after the accident. I ran my finger along the edge of the wood. The painted images of blue waves, red flames, green trees, and white clouds represented the earth's magical elements. With a frown, I yanked my finger back, slammed that line of thinking to a halt, and focused on my purpose.

A niggling thought at the back of my mind told me *Forbidden Island* would begin filming tonight, but I wanted to confirm that. And the location. This might be one of those rare occasions when an agent visited a set. If Jackson McKee was a cameraman on the movie, unless he was shooting b-roll elsewhere, he would be there.

I sighed when I called up the production information. Mia Fynn was producing. She wasn't a bad person – well, nixie, actually, a water spirit – but we just didn't get along. To be honest, I didn't get along with anybody in this town. Yet another drawback of being tied to a demon. I shrugged. It was what it was. Although I was beginning to wonder if I could change that.

The cast list drew my focus. I groaned. Besides my actors, the Paranormal Talent Agency represented several others. Its real name was the Peterson Talent Agency, but once it started catering to the other-than-human acting crowd, the nickname stuck. I saw Catherine's boyfriend, Alex the half-incubus, on the list, as well as Evie, the vampire, and her human boyfriend, Ryan.

The possibility of running into any of them didn't thrill me. Barbara had sent me to cross paths with them enough in the past. I distinctly remembered the time Evie outed me as a demon's minion to Catherine; such a sarcastic vampire. And then (unfortunately, but accurately) called me out for not even knowing what my demon boss's plans were. My cheeks reddened at the unpleasant memory. Some things never changed; I still didn't know my boss's ultimate plan.

On the positive, I confirmed my belief that filming started tonight. I scanned for the address, saw it was near my Summerlin office. That was convenient. Checking my watch, I had two hours until night fall and call time for the shoot. Okay, this was good. I'd plan to be there, scope out this Jackson McKee.

And then what?
Kill him?

CHAPTER THREE

I tugged on the bottom of my fitted purple t-shirt, observing the frenzied activity on the set. Cones blocked off sections of the grocery store parking lot next to the park where tonight's scenes would be filmed. Despite the name *Forbidden Island*, the movie took place in Las Vegas. I hadn't read the script; something about the island being an analogy for the loneliness of living in a city surrounded by people but remaining apart. I wouldn't know anything about that.

Up ahead, set lights reflected off green hair pulled back in a ponytail. I inwardly sighed before heading in the nixie's direction. She turned at the sound of my footsteps. I didn't miss the downturn of her lips before she plastered a fake smile on her face.

"Hi, Robin, what can I do for you?" Mia Fynn asked, all fake-solicitous with her set visitor. Not that I was bitter.

"Hi, Mia. I wanted to check things out since I have a few actors on this movie."

Her eyebrows rose a fraction. She wasn't buying it, but I doubted she'd challenge me. "Of course, welcome," she said, her smile still not reaching her emerald eyes. "Let me know if you need anything." And with a small nod, she glided away.

I took in the controlled chaos. For anyone who's never been on a set, you have your director, assistant director, director of photography, camera folks, and actors (both lead and background, otherwise known as extras). Not to mention wardrobe, hair and makeup, and a bunch of others whose names I could never keep straight, even after five years in the business.

I spotted a portly gentleman hoisting a camera and decided to begin there. I crossed the park, passing in and out of the artificial lights, my sneakers making whisper sounds in the grass.

"Excuse me? I'm looking for Jackson McKee," I said to the back of the man carrying the camera.

He turned, a quizzical look on his face. "Jackson?" Confusion cleared from his blue eyes. "Oh, do you mean Jack?"

"Maybe? I've never met him," I confided. "I'm Robin Landon of Landon Talent. I was told to find him on set."

"Gotcha." He hefted his body in a circle, scouting the crowd. He stopped and pointed. "See that man by the

RED 8K." I scanned until I saw the man standing beside the expensive camera on a tripod. "That's Jack."

I nodded and smiled. "Thanks."

"No problem."

I considered the backside of Jackson McKee as I approached him. He had close-cut brown hair and wore an Imagine Dragons t-shirt stretched tight across well-defined muscles, over jeans molded to a very fine backside indeed. Heat suffused my face.

Not good, thinking naughty thoughts about the man I was supposed to kill. That sobered me instantly. I stopped about five feet from him.

"Hi, can I help you?" His chocolate brown eyes searched mine.

"Um," I rather eloquently responded.

Jackson McKee took a few steps toward me. "Are you okay? Do you need something?"

Only a few inches taller than me and probably late-twenties like me, he radiated coiled strength. He rubbed his jaw, my mind hearing the scrape of his fingers against the stubble, wanting to brush my fingers across it too. My eyes widened at this instant attraction.

Jackson's smile faltered. "Ma'am?"

Ma'am? What was I, his mother? I strode forward, hand outstretched. "Hi, I'm Robin Landon of Landon Talent."

His hand closed around mine and held a second longer than customary. His eyes searched my face again. What did he see in my brown eyes that had him so curious? I'd been told often enough through the body language of others that I was a humdrum plain-Jane. Instantly forgettable, someone once said. But Jackson didn't look at me that way. Not like a frump in jeans with her shoulder-length brown hair in an unassuming pony tail.

"Hello, Robin Landon of Landon Talent," he responded formally.

I burst out laughing.

Jackson released my hand and smiled. "What can I do for you, Robin?"

"I'm just checking out the set."

He stared at me. Yeah, he caught that the answer made no sense, given I had asked for him by name. He appeared to let it go. "Well, then, welcome to the set." He shrugged. "Did you want to see something in particular?"

You with your shirt off, my mind shouted. I blushed again. Good grief, this was ridiculous.

He smirked and I wondered if the blush was visible in the low lighting. Man, I hoped not. I wasn't sure how I expected this first meeting to go, but this was not it.

"Nope," I finally answered his question. "Just poking around." That, at least, was true.

"Okay. I guess let me know if you need anything," he said, uncertainty in his voice.

"I will, thanks," I responded brightly then turned before I shoved my foot any further in my mouth. Did I hear him chuckling as I walked away? What a great first impression. Wait. Why was I trying to make a good impression? That ran completely counter to my goal. I groaned aloud.

"Robin, are you okay?"

I sarcastically thanked the universe for increasing the awkwardness of the evening and turned to face Catherine Rodham. Her long blond hair curled down around her shoulders and her blue eyes expressed concern. Huh, that concern was new. Catherine and her Paranormal Talent Agency friends were always so rude to me. I didn't know how to answer her. Part of me wanted to blurt out the whole sordid mess. I sighed instead. "I'll be fine. Thanks."

If my genuine appreciation surprised her, she hid it well. "Okay, you seem off, is all," she continued.

I almost wanted to take offense. But, I worked for a demon. What did I expect? "I'm trying to get a handle on something," I said. She was an empath of a sort. A magical human lie detector, I'd learned. She'd sense if I lied.

"I know we haven't been friendly," she said, "but if you ever need anything."

Both of us looked shocked by her offer and I smiled. "Thank you. I appreciate that."

She nodded and moved away, her face still expressing uncertainty. She wasn't alone. She and her friends always just tolerated me. Maybe I could ask them—

I shut down that thought. Barbara would be none too happy if I involved anybody else. And she had spies everywhere. She'd find out, for sure. I let that possibility go. Permanently.

With unexpected clarity, a plan came to me. I searched the crowd for Jackson again. A thrill of desire snaked through me when I saw him. He was laughing at something a fellow crew member was saying. His perfect white teeth flashed in a captivating smile. I made my way to him.

"Hello again, Robin Landon of Landon Talent," he greeted me.

"Hi, cameraman Jackson McKee," I responded in kind. We both grinned.

"Would you like to have breakfast or lunch with me tomorrow?" I blurted out the question before I could talk myself out of it. I didn't know if this was a good idea, but it was all I could come up with. Get close to him and... what? I'd figure it out as I went.

His eyes widened in surprise. I braced myself for the rejection. "I would love to," he accepted and my jaw dropped open. "Did you think I'd say no?"

"Um," I shook my head, "I didn't know."

"Give me your phone." I handed it to him. He entered his information. "Send me a text so I'll have your number. We'll go to BabyStacks for brunch, if that works for you."

Our eyes met and I swore something flared. Desire? This was a dangerous path I'd started down. I ignored the foreboding now flooding through me.

"It definitely works for me."

# CHAPTER FOUR

I kicked myself for arriving at BabyStacks so early. There was no traffic to speak of and I zipped along Buffalo Drive toward Desert Shores. My heart fluttered when I saw Jackson standing just inside the front door by the hostess station. I scanned the cozy restaurant décor, noting the red-brick-style flooring and natural wood and stone accents throughout. My eyes returned to Jackson. He again wore a pair of jeans and a concert t-shirt. How was he not cold? It was probably his uniform style. I smoothed out nonexistent wrinkles from my purple long-sleeved fitted shirt over leggings and boots.

"Guess I wasn't the only one eager for brunch," he quipped and I chuckled. "I've already put my name on the list. When I saw how early I was, I figured I'd go ahead and do so. That way you wouldn't have had to wait at all," he explained.

"That was very gentlemanly of you."

"I try."

We smiled at each other.

"Jack, party of two?" The hostess broke the spell. We followed her to a two-top table next to a stone wall. Jackson pulled my chair out.

"Thank you," I murmured. He took the wooden chair opposite. We watched each other as the hostess placed menus in front of us. "The hostess called you Jack. Do you prefer that to Jackson?"

A half-smile flitted on his face. "Normally I do, but I like the way you say Jackson."

"You do?" I asked with a flirty smile back.

"I do." His voice sounded huskier.

"Okay, then. Jackson." We stared at each other. I rubbed my lips together; his eyes followed the movement with interest. Okay, then, indeed! I opened up the menu.

"Have you been here before?" Jackson asked.

"I haven't. I assume you have since you picked it."

"I have, but it's been awhile. The pancakes are awesome, as you'd expect by the name."

"I'll have to try some."

After that scintillating exchange, the conversation lulled while we perused the menu and surreptitiously checked the other out. He still had his five o'clock shadow; it worked for him, highlighting the contours of his jawline and kissable lips.

Kissable? I inwardly rolled my eyes. Time to focus on why I asked him out. Not just because I found him sweet and insanely attractive.

"How long have you been a cameraman?"

"A few years. I tried acting first, believe it or not, and hated it."

"You hated it?"

"Turned out I didn't enjoy the audition process."

"I don't think anybody does."

"True. But I also didn't enjoy memorizing lines."

My brow furrowed. "Why did you want to be an actor at all then?"

He laughed, low and sexy. "I didn't, to be honest. A photographer told me I had the look for it and I thought it might be fun."

I echoed his laughter. "You definitely have the look," I said. An instant flush crept up my neck. He quirked an eyebrow. "I'm a talent agent. It's my job to notice."

He nodded, but the twinkle in his eyes told me he didn't buy my explanation.

"It's too tough a business if you aren't committed," I added.

"Exactly. I did, however, discover that I enjoyed watching the cameramen. So, I took some classes, did some student films, and ta da, now I'm a full-time cameraman. What about you? How long have you been a talent agent?"

My smile fell and I swallowed past the lump in my throat. How to explain that I got my agency by signing a pact with a demon?

"Hey, it's okay," he said with concern, reaching to take one of my hands in his. "We're just getting to know each other. If it's not something you want to talk about—"

I rolled my eyes, tried to laugh off the awkwardness. "That's a long boring story." I pulled my hand from his when the waitress appeared to take our order.

His eyes stayed on me as I purposefully kept my own on the waitress. She took the order and departed. I dropped my gaze to my lap. I needed to get this conversation back on track.

"Tell me about the others on set."

Jackson took my conversational redirect in stride and regaled me with his histories with various members of the crew. Slowly the conversation became loose and fun. So, of course, I realized it was time to make it weird again. I needed to remember my goal.

"Do you know Barbara Knollman?"

"The Councilwoman?"

"Yes, that's her."

He shrugged. "I know of her. I've seen her on *Entertainment Daily* but I've never met her." He tilted his head. "Why do you ask?"

"Are you sure?"

"Yes. Why?" He frowned slightly.

I needed to say something but my thoughts swirled in consternation. Why would Barbara want him dead if he had never met her? Could he have done something he wasn't aware of?

"Why do you ask if I know the councilwoman?"

I decided to provide part of the truth. "I sometimes do work for her," I started vaguely. "Anyway, she mentioned you the other day."

Understanding dawned in his eyes, but there was an undercurrent of something unreadable. He knew more than he was saying, I'd bet money on it. "That's why you were checking me out on set?"

"I wasn't checking you out," I disagreed. He grinned. "Okay, I was checking you out. But you were checking me out, too," I reminded him.

He laughed. "Yes, I was. I freely admit that."

"Why?" The question slipped out before I could stop it. Ugh. That sounded pathetic.

Again, the inscrutable expression, though his face quickly smoothed out. "There's something about you, Robin."

My jaw dropped open and I snapped it shut. This hunk of a man thought there was something about shy, unassuming me? That blew my mind.

Not that I had low self-esteem or anything, but I understood my strengths. Physical beauty wasn't one of them.

I redirected the conversation back to safer ground and the rest of the breakfast passed as expected. For the life of me, I could not understand why Barbara wanted this man dead. When Jackson walked me to my car and hugged me goodbye, promising to call, I made my mind up.

I would challenge the demon.

## CHAPTER FIVE

"What did you say?" Barbara Knollman's icy tone clashed with her fiery eyes. Did I smell brimstone? I clamped down on my overactive imagination, ignored the acid burning a hole in my stomach. I lifted my chin and met her hard stare.

"You heard me." The calm in my voice amazed me. I willed my poker face to stay in place. "Unless you can give me a good answer to why you want Jackson McKee dead, I refuse to kill him."

The demon's red eyes slowly returned to their normal obsidian. Fathomless black holes, I sometimes thought. I withstood the urge to shudder. Barbara smiled, her small, pointed teeth unnerving as always. She stood and leaned over her desk.

"You are not in a position to refuse," she responded, her reasonable tone belying the steel beneath.

"Yes, I am," I retorted. "What's the worst you can do?"

Barbara lifted a single eyebrow.

My cheeks reddened. Well, yeah, she could probably damn me to hell for all eternity. I shook my head. "It doesn't matter," I insisted. "I'm not a killer."

"Now I'm confused." She retook her seat, the fabric of her pants whispering as she crossed her legs with deliberate slowness. "Either you aren't willing to kill him at all or you're only willing to kill him for a good reason. Which is it?"

Her saccharine tone chilled me. "He doesn't even know you," I redirected. "None of this makes any sense."

Barbara sighed, startling me. "Fine."

"Really?"

"Not that I owe you an explanation," she continued. "But my visions showed me that his death is necessary."

"For what?"

"For me to achieve my goal."

"What goal?" I couldn't believe how belligerent and demanding I was being. Did I have a death wish this morning?

"That is not information I plan on sharing." Barbara stared placidly at me, waiting for my response. I considered it for a half minute, made a show of considering my options.

"That's not good enough." I took a deep, steadying breath, which did not go unnoticed by the demon, who sneered.

"It's not?" Her tone remained light, but I didn't buy it.

"No. It's not. I refuse to kill anyone. For any reason."

She tilted her head.

"That wasn't in our agreement," I added, hoping to find an end-run around her demand.

"Are you sure, minion?"

I hesitated. No, I wasn't sure. I had been in such a low place when I made the deal. I didn't remember much about what I had signed in blood. That was bad, right?

"I gather from your silence that you realize the folly of refusing?"

Goosebumps rose on my arms. I opened my mouth. How much longer would I live after uttering this next phrase? "I do – and I choose to do so anyway. I refuse to kill anyone. Do what you will."

I felt defeated and yet free. She might smite me down, or something like that, but at least I would leave this world not a killer. I gripped the sides of the chair, feared how much it would hurt.

"Okay," Barbara responded with a nod. "You won't kill him."

That rendered me speechless. I released my death grip and tried a small smile. "Thank you?"

"You may leave now," she said, her black eyes flat.

I darted from the room, pleased, but wary. The smarter part of me understood I missed something important. I had to have.

There was no way the demon would allow me to defy her like that.

## CHAPTER SIX

An invitation the next day from Jackson almost distracted me from my terrified waiting-for-the-other-shoe-to-drop feeling. Almost. He had texted with a late invite to dinner. Although he apologized for the last minute text, I understood the unpredictability of a movie shoot.

I stood now before the full-length mirror hanging on the back of my closet door, evaluating my outfit choice. The weather was mild for December and I thought I could get away with wearing a long-sleeve shirt dress over leggings without a jacket. I kept my hair in its serviceable ponytail and skipped makeup.

He seemed to like me for me, so I wasn't going to mess with that. A quick check of my watch told me he would arrive soon.

Sure enough, the doorbell chimed, and I crossed the stone floor from the bedroom through the living room. My breath caught in my throat when I opened the front door. Jackson looked yummy. My gaze traveled the length of him, from his fitted navy blue button-down shirt to his dark jeans and cowboy boots. His permanent five o'clock shadow begged to be touched. He smiled at my clear appreciation, skin crinkling around his eyes.

"You look beautiful," he greeted me.

"Thanks, so do you."

He held his arm out, and I allowed him to lead me to his car, actually a Ford F150 truck. I must have made a noise.

"Yeah, the truck's big," he said. "I like to go camping, plus it's good for lugging camera equipment around." He opened the door and helped me into the cab.

I was rarely in bigger vehicles; I felt incredibly high up. The feeling triggered a giggle. Jackson glanced at me inquisitively. I shook my head.

"Just marveling at the view from up here."

We drove the short bit on South Town Center Drive and turned onto West Charleston Avenue, heading for Red Rock Casino. It was a great complex off-Strip, including a movie theater and bowling alley.

But, we were headed to 8 Noodle Bar, an Asian fusion restaurant, for dinner. Busy for a weeknight, Jackson maneuvered his behemoth toward the back of a parking lot, near a parking lot light. The dark mountains rose in the distance beyond the casino.

Jackson hurried around the front of the truck to open my door and help me down. Our eyes locked and a thrill raced through me.

"Are you hungry?"

My jaw dropped at his double entendre. I failed to respond around the cotton balls in my mouth.

He chuckled. "I meant for food."

"Of course."

"At least right now," he teased.

I threaded my arm through his. Before we took two steps, he tensed. I stole a glance at him, wondering what had changed. His eyes had a glassy, far-away look. He slammed to a halt, causing me to stumble. He remained silent. With small movements, he assessed our surroundings.

Anxiety fluttered in my chest. "Jackson? What's wrong?"

He didn't respond. I looked around, trying to identify the source of his concern. Nothing jumped out. Parked cars. A few people approaching the casino in the distance. Everything seemed normal.

You know how they say, in times of stress, things move fast yet slow. Turned out that was accurate.

I glanced up at the parking lot light illuminating us.

A loud pop broke the silence.

Jackson threw me to the ground, his body shielding mine.

A dome of glowing light shimmered like a force field around us.

Glass shards from the light fixture bounced off the air above us. The lighting unit itself followed. I uttered a choked scream and flung my hands over my head, but the unit bounced harmlessly off the shimmering light and crashed to the ground beside where we huddled.

My brain struggled to process what happened. That falling light could have killed us, probably should have. How did we not get hit? What was that weird shimmering light surrounding us?

Jackson shot to his feet, pulling me with him. He seemed satisfied by whatever he saw when he stared into the darkness before hurrying to the truck. He yanked open my door.

"Get in," he ordered, before running around to his side of the truck.

The tires squealed when he backed up. We roared through the lot. Once on Charleston, I risked speaking. "What happened back there?" The silence stretched and I wondered if he would answer.

"Someone tried to hurt us."

"That wasn't just an accident?"

He glanced at me, worry etched across his face. "No."

## CHAPTER SEVEN

"How do you know?" I asked.

Jackson turned the truck onto South Town Center Drive. "I felt an energy change."

"What do you mean?"

"Someone caused that light to fall."

Acid pooled in my belly. Someone tried to kill us? Barbara's flat smile and obsidian eyes flashed in my mind. "Who would do that?" I asked instead.

"Someone with telekinesis."

"Telekinesis? You mean, someone moved the light with their mind?"

"Yes."

"A witch?" I squeaked the question, unsure how he'd respond.

He glanced at me again, expression unreadable. "Maybe."

"Did you keep the light from hitting us?"

He entered the code to open my small community's security gate. "Yes," he answered. We watched the security arm rise.

"Are you a witch?" Even though the overall supernatural underworld had been outed a few months ago, most supernatural beings still preferred not to announce their presence to the world.

He kept his head straight, looking ahead and not at me. "Yes."

"You have telekinesis, too?"

He startled at that and then nodded understanding at what I was asking. "No. I have protection magic."

"You created a personal shield for us?"

We pulled into my driveway and he killed the engine. He turned to face me. "Something like that," he said with a brief smile. "We need to get into the house and off the street."

We exited the vehicle and hastened up the walkway to enter my single-story stucco home. Once I locked the door behind us, my racing heart rate calmed to closer to normal.

"Would you like something to drink?"

Jackson released a breath I hadn't realized he was holding. "Yeah. That would be great."

I indicated he could sit on the chocolate-brown loveseat in my small living room and stepped into the kitchen opposite. "Wine okay? I have both white and red."

"Red would be great."

I poured us each a glass of Merlot. I could hear Jackson moving around. He was at the bay window overlooking the street when I returned to the living room. I paused, shaken at the sight of him standing off to the side, peering through the blinds, guessing from the movies he was trying to make himself a smaller target. A lump formed in my throat. This was all my fault.

"Here's the wine," I announced and set the glasses down on the coffee table in front of the loveseat. Jackson glanced at me before returning to stare out the window. His body tensed when I approached him, which confused me. I hesitantly touched his shoulder. "Hey. Come sit down."

He didn't respond, so I reached to take his hand in mine. "Let's talk about what happened." He nodded and I led him to the loveseat.

We both grabbed our wine like it was water in a desert and took large gulps. Jackson met my eyes. "What do you think happened?"

The demon tried to kill you? "I'm not sure," I hedged. "What do *you* think happened? How did you know that light was going to fall?"

"Part of my ability comes with an increased sensitivity to the use of magic around me. Right after we started walking, I picked up an energy source."

"What kind of energy source?"

"I wasn't sure at first. That's why I stopped walking. I needed to focus on identifying where the mounting energy was coming from. I didn't know if it was intended for harm initially, but then I knew it was being directed toward us."

"How?"

He gave me a lop-sided smile. "That's the million dollar question, I suppose. I can feel it and just sort of know where it'll be sent." He shrugged. "That's all I got."

"So then you used your... protection magic?"

"Once I knew it was coming, yes."

"That's when you erected the force field. Or shield? What would you call it?"

He chuckled. "Either of those works. I imagined a barrier between us and the magic, and then it was there."

"Protecting us from both the magic itself and the resulting damaged light falling?" I broke eye contact with him as I pondered. My gut feeling that Barbara hadn't just accepted my refusal to kill Jackson must have been correct. Who was this new person? A replacement killer?

"What are you thinking?"

I resumed eye contact, striving to keep my face a blank. This would be the perfect time to explain my defunct-witch status. But how to begin?

"You don't seem very surprised." Although said in a neutral tone, I felt the question poking around the words.

"I saw Elizabeth Addison's expose on *Entertainment Daily*," I offered by way of explanation and it worked.

Jackson laughed. "Yeah, I thought that reporter did a number on us with her morning show. But, I was wrong."

"You were?"

He shrugged. "Despite her big exposé and continuing coverage, nothing's really changed for any of us, day to day."

"Mm-hmm." Barbara had predicted we'd be brought to light, and she also wasn't surprised it hadn't become a big deal. None of which I could say to Jackson.

Jackson tilted his head. "What?"

"Just wondering why someone would want to hurt one or both of us."

His expression hardened. "I intend to find out." He placed a hand on my knee. "It'll be okay. Normally I'd say since I'm a witch, I was the target."

No kidding. "Are you going to be okay?"

"I'll talk to the head of the Witches Council about what happened."

"There's a real Witches Council?" Even though I was a nonfunctioning witch, I knew about the Witches Council. But I couldn't acknowledge it without telling him about me – and about Barbara and her order. Not until I understood what was happening.

Jackson squeezed my knee. "That reporter doesn't know the half of what goes on in this town."

"No doubt. Wait a minute," I interrupted myself. "You said 'normally' you'd believe you were the target?"

"You could be the target," he admitted.

"What? Why?" My questioning tone only partly feigned.

"I could tell my magic was drawn to protect you from the first moment I saw you. There's usually a reason."

"Oh." An ugly thought reared its head and my hands formed fists. Disappointment bubbled at the idea that he wasn't interested in me, that I'd misread his protection magic as romantic intentions.

"You're going to be fine," he assured me, misinterpreting.

I uncurled my fingers. "I'm sure I will," I murmured. "You probably need to go. So you can start investigating." I rose and he stood awkwardly beside me.

His eyes showed confusion. "Probably. Rain check?"

I half-smiled. "Absolutely. Call me?"

"I will."

I strode past him toward the front door. We stood in the open doorway for a moment. "Okay," he said. "I'll let you know what I find out."

I nodded, feeling like a bobblehead, but not trusting myself to speak.

Jackson leaned in to hug me, careful not to get too close as my arms limply went around him. Confusion practically radiated off him. I couldn't blame him but I couldn't banish that ugly thought.

I closed the door, listened to the truck's engine roar to life and then fade as he moved further and further away.

A single tear slid down my cheek and I returned to the loveseat, picked my wine glass back up. I downed the rest in one large swallow and considered what I had learned. The ugly thought had told me the truth. Now I understood Jackson's interest. He had never been interested in me for me. It was his magic telling him I needed protection.

I remembered our brief encounters. He sure seemed to be into me. Could I have misread his intent all along? I was so confused. Well, just like I told Jackson, investigation was the next step.

I headed to the kitchen for more wine fortification. I'd need it if I was going to challenge the demon. Again.

# CHAPTER EIGHT

The déjà vu was strong today. I sat before Barbara Knollman in her office, once again gripping the sides of the leather chair like my life depended on it. Light streamed through the window behind her, the warmth not penetrating the chill on my skin.

Barbara stared at me, dark eyes revealing nothing. Her hair was pulled back in its typical severe bun and her hands rested on her desk. Waiting.

I swallowed past the lump in my throat. It was now or never. "Did you hire someone else to kill Jackson?"

Barbara blinked then slowly smiled. The predator visible beneath the calm exterior. "To kill Jackson?"

Her question-as-answer confused me. "Yes?"

"Are you sure it was a single target?"

Barbara's not so cryptic response floored me. "You were trying to kill us both?"

Barbara held both hands up. "I did nothing to you; I wasn't there," she denied. "Be careful what accusations you throw around without proof, Ms. Landon."

"You hired a replacement killer?!" My mind buzzed. She tried to kill us. In retrospect, I wasn't truly surprised. She already wanted Jackson dead; she merely added me for refusing to complete the job.

Barbara shrugged. "I did nothing to you."

"Are you saying it was just a coincidence?"

"Choices have consequences."

That was the closest I was likely to get to an admission that the demon tried to kill me. "Now what?" I voiced the biggest question rumbling around in my mind.

Barbara remained quiet, her eyes focused over my shoulder. Thinking. "We may be coming to the end of our relationship."

"You're releasing me from my pact?"

A cruel smile played on her lips. "That isn't what I said."

"Oh."

Her gaze drilled a hole through me. "We may be coming to the end of our relationship," she repeated.

"Am I going to hell?" I whispered.

Barbara shocked me by belly laughing. "Not yet."

Thank goodness! "What does this mean?" I asked.

"You ask so many questions you already know the answer to." She flicked her hand toward the door. "Leave."

I did.

*****

Knowing that Barbara had put a price on my head, the truth slammed home. This was much bigger than I could handle alone. I would need reinforcements. One name came to mind.

I tried to come up with an alternative option during the drive back to my house. I parked my car in the driveway and rested my forehead on the steering wheel. Nothing. Nobody else I knew had any experience dealing with the supernatural, and Barbara specifically. I sighed.

Once inside, I sat at the high-top kitchen table, running my hands along the smooth dark wood surface. Delaying. I knew that. Placing this next call would be harder in some ways even than challenging the demon. What if she refused to help?

I placed my cellphone on the table in front of me, spinning it, straightening it up, fidgeting. I sighed again. Just get it over with. Unlike with Barbara, the worst she could do was say no.

Before I could talk myself out of it, I snatched the phone up and made the call.

"Catherine Rodham speaking."

I found myself unable to respond to the voice of the talent agent on the other end.

"Hello? Is someone there?"

"Catherine," I croaked out.

Crickets on her end.

"Catherine?"

"Robin, is that you?" Disgust curled around each syllable.

"I need your help."

Crickets again. Oh, good grief, this was like sticks under my fingernails.

"Please." I closed my eyes.

A small sigh and then she offered a ray of hope. "How can I help?"

CHAPTER NINE

Despite her reluctance, Catherine was true to her word. She sat with her Paranormal Talent Agency friends in a private booth at the back of *Soprannaturale*. A were-panther from Italy owned the hole-in-the-wall paranormal café; hence the name, Italian for supernatural. It was on a dead-end street off Main Street, such that non-supernatural beings were unlikely to stumble upon it. Although, ever since the paranormal underworld had been thrown into the spotlight, hordes of Vegas tourists had made it their missions to find supernatural hotspots. But, so far, the luck of the café had held steady and none had found it.

I could count on one hand the number of times I'd gone. Being a demon's minion meant I was not exactly welcome. A few patrons glared at me when I stepped into the café out of the cool evening. Vampires had pushed two tables together; their fangs descended halfway and four sets of eyes stared at me like I was now on the menu. I swore I heard growls from where two werewolves with amber eyes sat at a table farther inside. When I saw two older witches whisper a possible incantation in my direction, it confirmed my undesirability.

But I guessed it was true about having connected friends. Nobody approached me or challenged me. Even the owner, the hunky were-panther, Antonio DiMaio, simply observed me dispassionately, chocolate brown eyes hooded. I passed the scattered Formica-covered two-top tables, avoiding eye contact and focusing on the guild-framed canvases depicting lovely pastoral scenes from Italy.

I stood awkwardly at the table, staring at the booth's forest green vinyl upholstery instead of faces, trying not to wince at the hostility emanating from the women already seated. Well, to be fair, only one woman radiated open hostility.

"Hi, Evie," I greeted the vampire. Maybe I could defuse her irritation. Her blue eyes narrowed to slits and she shook her head, blond curls bouncing. Turned in the 1920s, Evie Jones was now an actress who kept that signature style.

"Please, sit, Robin," Mia Fynn said kindly. The nixie's green hair was pulled into a ponytail like my own, and her emerald eyes reflected openness with a dash of wariness. I nodded and slid in next to Catherine, ignoring the way she tensed at the movement. Who was I kidding? I knew they wouldn't make this easy.

I sighed. "Thank you, Catherine," I directed my opening remarks at the empath. "And thank you, Mia and Evie. For agreeing to meet with me." My gaze dropped to my hands fidgeting in my lap. Tears threatened to overflow.

"Why are we here?" Evie demanded.

"Now, Evie, give her a chance," Mia soothed, her musical nixie voice washing over the table, calming us all with her magic.

"You said you needed my help?" Catherine prompted.

"Yes." Best to jump right in. "You know me as Barbara Knollman's minion. The demon's minion. And that's true. I made a deal with the demon in the past." How much to tell them? My mouth chose not to form the words, 'I am a witch'. "I've mostly been her gopher, as you have pointed out before. For the first time, though, she asked something of me that I refused to do."

"I didn't think there was anything off limits for a minion," Evie said.

My cheeks reddened. "It's never come up before."

Evie shrugged. "You reap what you sow."

"I know. And I would understand if you didn't want to help me."

"Gee, I'm glad you're so understanding," Evie said.

"Evie!" Catherine said.

"What? Why are we sitting here like we don't have history with this minion." Evie sat forward, pointed a finger at me. "You've always been a lackey. Why would we want to help you with a problem you're having with your demon?"

"Since you're here, I assumed—" I stopped and looked around the table. Two sets of hooded eyes and one vampire set still narrowed in suspicion.

"What does she want you to do?" Catherine asked. We hadn't discussed the specifics when I called her; she'd preferred to wait and include the ladies in the conversation.

"She wants me to kill someone."

Catherine and Mia gasped. "Why am I not surprised?" Evie said.

"Who does she want you to kill?" Mia asked.

"Jackson McKee." At their blank expressions, I explained, "He's a cameraman on *Forbidden Island.*"

"Did she tell you why she wants him dead?" Catherine asked.

I shook my head. "She didn't, except that it would help her achieve her 'goal'. And, before you ask, she wouldn't tell me her goal."

Catherine tapped her fingers on the table top. "Anything else?"

I bit my lower lip. What I was about to say was Jackson's secret to disclose. But he would surely understand I was trying to save his life. "He's a witch."

The ladies didn't even appear shocked.

"He must be some kind of threat to her," Evie guessed.

"I don't think so. His magic is protection magic."

"How do you know that?" Catherine asked.

An image of a lighting fixture falling toward my head flashed in my mind and ribbons of anxiety snaked through me. "Barbara tried to kill us. Jackson used his magic to prevent it."

Again, the gasps of surprise, Evie included this time. "Because you refused to kill him?" she asked.

Was that respect I saw in her eyes? Would wonders never cease? I nodded.

"And she got someone else to do the job?" Evie asked, her disgust now aimed at the demon.

I nodded again.

"How can we help?" Mia asked.

"I'm not sure. I'd like to find and stop this replacement killer." I looked around for water, realized none had been ordered. "I think it's unrealistic to also stop Barbara, but," I exhaled in a rush, "I'd like to at least break the pact before she sends me to hell."

Catherine gently placed her hand on my arm. "We'll do whatever we can." She looked at the other two. "Right, ladies?"

"Absolutely," Mia responded.

Evie quirked an eyebrow, then sighed. "Yeah, I'm in, too."

Relief surged through me. "Thank you all so much." Tears threatened again. "I don't know what to say."

Catherine frowned. "Why isn't Jackson here? Since he's part of the supernatural world and he's the target."

"I'm trying to protect him," I hedged my response. "The less he knows, the better."

"That's it?" Catherine pressed. I had no doubt her magical lie detector was pinging at the incompleteness of my answer.

"I'd just rather he stays away from this as much as possible," I demurred.

Catherine stared at me for a beat. I could practically see her mind file my non-answer for future consideration. "Let's brainstorm. What should be our first step?"

"I would think we need to convince Barbara to cancel the second killer," Evie offered with a slight lift of her right shoulder.

"That's not a bad idea," Mia agreed.

"Thoughts on how?" Catherine asked.

My heart filled with hope as I watched these three women figuring out how to save my life. I could see a faint light at the end of that tunnel everyone talked about.

Soon we had a plan.

The first step? Heading back into the lion's den – or rather, the demon's office. Again.

# CHAPTER TEN

I sat in the all-too-familiar leather chair in Barbara's office. The day that I wouldn't have to sit here could not come soon enough. She looked up from her desk. "We need to stop meeting like this."

Was that a joke? Thrown for a moment, I didn't respond.

The demon rolled her eyes. "What can I do for you, Ms. Landon?"

Lying to the non-supernatural was easy; my years in foster care had honed that ability. Supernatural folks, well, I never knew what magical abilities they possessed. "I've changed my mind." I tensed, waiting for her response.

A single eyebrow raised. "About what?"

"Handling that problem we discussed."

My skin crawled as her gaze bore into me. "To what exactly are you referring?"

"I learned my lesson and will do your bidding as agreed." My chin dropped a fraction, like the obedient minion I desperately needed to convince her I still was. "I will kill Jackson McKee." I flinched from an imagined attack response and Barbara smirked. This was going swimmingly. Ugh.

"Will you now?"

"Yes."

"Wonderful."

I breathed a small sigh of relief.

"I truly hope you succeed first."

Wait. What? "First?"

"When we initially discussed this problem, I gave you a week to solve it. When you then expressed concern a day later about being able to do so, I contracted out with a different problem-solver. Another two days have passed. That leaves three remaining," she added, like I was a child who couldn't do basic math. She shrugged. "Whoever gets the job done first."

Thoughts swirled in my mind. She watched me. She was waiting to see if I would beg. After five years, I recognized the futility of that. I controlled my rising panic. The first part of the plan had gone down in flames. On to the next…

"I understand," I responded. "Toward that, I decided to go with unconventional resources."

Barbara sat back in her chair, hands folded in front of her.

"I approached Catherine Rodham of the Paranormal Talent Agency—"

Another eye roll. Barbara was in rare form today. "I know who she is."

I stared straight into her obsidian eyes. Please don't turn red. "I've told them I'm acting against you, to secure their assistance with… solving the problem." This was such a huge risk. The women and I had decided I should stay with one of them or Jackson at all times until this resolved, to remain safe. Being upfront in this way, while baldly lying, had been my idea.

She bristled then smoothed out her features. "Interesting."

That was it? "Thank you?"

"I know they hate me," she said. "No doubt they were only too happy to sign on to get back at me. I trust you have a plan that benefits from their assistance." She held up a hand to stop me from responding. "That was a rhetorical statement. I don't actually care." Her stare glued me to my chair. "We'll see within three days. Won't we?" Barbara stood.

My eyes, of their own volition, furtively checked to learn if today was the day I'd finally glimpse the demon's tail. It wasn't. I bit down hard on the side of my cheek to keep a crazed giggle from escaping, as I didn't have a death wish.

Honest.

*****

"Do you want the good news first, or the bad news?" I asked, without preamble. I hadn't even left the parking lot of the city council building before placing the call to Catherine.

"Good news, I guess."

"Barbara bought my story of you guys helping me as a way to stick it to her."

Catherine snort laughed. "Of course, she did. She knows we don't like or trust her. Hit me with the bad news."

I ran my free hand around my steering wheel to delay.

"Robin? Are you still there? It's not that bad, is it?"

"The first part of the plan was a complete bust."

She gasped. "You're not saying what I think you're saying?"

I nodded though she couldn't see me. "Yep. Barbara isn't calling off the second killer."

Silence on the line. I waited it out. "Okay. That's a blow," Catherine began. "But, let's look at it as extra motivation."

My eyebrows shot upward. "Extra motivation? Staying alive was already my motivation." I gave a shaky chuckle. "Though now it's being threatened from multiple sources. So, I guess you're right."

"I'll let Evie and Mia know what happened. With the replacement killer still in play, it's even more important to learn what Jackson got from the Witches Council. Has he met with them yet?"

At Catherine's use of his name, my heart lurched. "I don't know. I haven't spoken with him since we hammered out our plan."

"That needs to be next on the list."

"I'll call him as soon as I hang up the phone."

"Is that all?"

"What do you mean?"

A nearly imperceptible sigh from Catherine. "Your responses are reading as incomplete," she admitted.

I cursed under my breath. "You and your magical lie detector – I can't get anything past you," I half-joked.

She waited.

"I'm hesitant to call him. But, I will."

"Why are you hesitant?"

"I thought there might be something between us. Romantically. It was obviously only his protection magic."

"While I haven't seen you two together, I have experience in this realm. Just take it one day at a time and try not to read too much into it."

"I don't know," I said slowly.

"Look at it this way. The whole thing will be over in three days. And if neither of you is dead by then," she added in a sing-song voice, "you can see if there might be something there."

I smiled. "You're right. I have to get over myself."

"That's not quite what I meant," Catherine said with a laugh.

"No, but that's the truth. I need to focus on everybody staying alive and breaking my pact with Barbara. Jackson is a critical part of that."

"That's my girl."

Catherine's comment left us speechless. I didn't have mind reading abilities, but I guessed she was as shocked as I was.

Were we becoming… friends?

"Meet at *Soprannaturale* when the sun sets?" She returned to business.

"I'll be there. And I'll let you know what I learn from Jackson." I disconnected and scrolled for Jackson's number. My mouth went dry listening to the ringing of the call.

"Hey, Robin," he answered.

Hearing my name said with his gruff voice sent tingles down my spine.

Oh my.

"Hey, Jackson." I coughed. "I was calling to see what you learned from the Witches Council about the being who attacked us."

"I haven't learned anything—"

The news crushed me. I had put so much hope into their collective knowledge.

"—because I haven't gone yet."

The words filtered through my brain. "I'm sorry, I might have missed something. You haven't gone yet?"

His warm laugh rolled over me. "No, I haven't. Would you like to come with me? I was about to head over. They're meeting this afternoon."

A confused variety of thoughts swirled. How well would I be able to balance not knowing if our attraction was real with keeping my secrets from him and finding a hired killer?

"Robin?"

Ah, screw it. Catherine was right. I needed to focus. Everything would sort itself out. "Text me the address and I'll meet you there."

"Wonderful. I'm really looking forward to seeing you."

"Me too. I'll see you soon." The call ended and an address appeared. My brow furrowed.

That location on Industrial Road was a business district; was that where the Witches Council met? On the plus side, it was only a short drive.

My heart hammered in my chest. I wanted the information on the hired killer. But I also had my private reason, the one I chose to hide from Jackson.

Would the witches be able to help me break my pact with Barbara?

And would they be able to help me with the secret I was keeping from even the ladies?

Help me unbind my powers?

And I'd be lying if I didn't admit I looked forward to seeing Jackson again, too.

# CHAPTER ELEVEN

The thought that I had only three more days to solve this mess swirled in my mind. I zipped my Jetta into a parking spot in front of a wide, squat metal-gray building. Definitely in the industrial part of town, thus the street name, I supposed. A quick glance around confirmed I beat Jackson here. That gave me time to consider my approach. I could roll with whatever he had planned for the Witches Council. But I'd also need to find somebody I could speak to on the down low about my personal issue. I smiled at myself in the rearview mirror. The down low? Like I was in a mystery novel or something.

Motion drew my attention. My breath caught in my throat. Jackson wore a dark brown pullover with jeans, muscles straining the material as he strode from my right, toward the front door. A man with purpose, but unhurried by anxiety. He must have sensed someone watching him;

he turned his head and our eyes met through the windshield. A wide smile lit his face and desire pooled low in my belly.

I exited my car, wondering about this reaction. It was his protection magic, right?

"Hey, Robin. Have you been waiting long?"

"Nah, a few minutes. Thanks for inviting me."

"You were there, too. Seems only fitting for you to be here." He held the door open for me to enter before him. Despite my immediate physical reaction to him, since deciding to let things progress as they would, I felt less anxiety talking to Jackson.

We entered the utilitarian foyer inches apart, a soft chime announcing our presence. With its linoleum flooring and hard plastic chairs, you'd never guess the Witches Council met here. I wondered how much time the members spent in this building.

A door at the back of the room opened and a woman approached. "Jackson, how great to see you. It's been a minute." A pang of jealousy hit me as they embraced. Good grief, the man can't have friends?

"Jessica, this is Robin. She was there when the incident occurred. Robin, this is Jessica. She's the newest liaison on the Council."

Late-twenties like me, Jessica had curly flames of red hair and bright brown eyes. She clasped my hand, her eyes searching mine. My smile faltered for a moment.

"It's nice to meet you, Robin."

"You as well, Jessica." I recovered from whatever that was and we followed Jessica through to the back.

"We're still waiting on Evan, but everyone else is here and ready," she called over her shoulder. We walked down a short hallway, stopping at a closed door on the left. Jessica knocked twice softly and then opened it to grant us entry.

This room belied what I had just seen. Antique wall sconces held electric lights that reflected off silvery wallpaper. Soft gray carpeting meant our steps remained silent. We crossed the mid-size room to a row of upscale folding chairs (was that even a thing?) facing a half-circle table with five chairs behind it. Three of these fancier chairs were occupied.

Jessica indicated we should sit in the folding chairs and she took a seat behind the table, next to two women and a man tapping away on their cellphones. "We'll get started as soon as Evan arrives."

My shoulders tightened with my heightened anxiety. Gaining information about the replacement killer was the top priority. But this was also the final part of the plan created with the Paranormal Talent Agency women: find someone here who could help me break the pact with Barbara and unbind my powers.

"So sorry I'm late," a male voice broke the silence. A tall, heavyset man nodded at us as he crossed to sit in the remaining open seat behind the table. "Have we done introductions?" he asked, glancing around. "I'm Evan. Welcome."

Jessica chuckled. "I guess we're jumping right in. Now you've met Evan. This is Matt" – she indicated an older bald gentleman – "Theresa" – a middle-aged blond with garish red lipstick – "and Marcie" – a young blond woman who barely looked out of her teens, but surely was older. "Welcome to the Witches Council."

"Thank you for seeing us," Jackson began. "I only wish it was under better circumstances." He brought them up to speed with what happened in the parking lot, including our uncertainty over who was the target, given that his protection magic seemed focused on me.

I tried not to squirm in my seat; this was the perfect opening to explain that we both were targets, and why, but I couldn't make my mouth form the words. I had to admit I didn't want Jackson to know I was a demon's minion. A sigh escaped and Jackson glanced questioningly at me. I smiled weakly in return before deliberately turning to look at the council members. Four of the five watched Jackson, but Jessica stared back at me. A flush crept up my neck. Did she know something? Sense something? Man, a room full of witches was a tough crowd!

Jackson had finished his recitation and taken his seat.

"Thank you for sharing with us," the middle-aged blond, Theresa, said. "We know that someone has begun using black magic in the city." A smudge of red lipstick on her front tooth drew my eye. I stared as she continued, distracted by the mark. "Unfortunately, we have been unable to pinpoint more specifically than that. Whoever is using it, is only using it in short bursts, and is able to throw up a mask almost immediately after." Theresa frowned.

The Council continued to discuss options, but I tuned them out when I realized they didn't have a clue what to do. Tracking the magic wasn't working because of the masking. And the witch wasn't using the magic often enough to try a stronger spell. After all, it had only been two days.

I felt eyes burning a hole in the side of my head and shifted to find Jessica staring at me again. No animosity in her expression, just curiosity. I had hoped to speak with someone at the Council without Jackson finding out. Based on her interest in me, Jessica became my first choice.

The meeting ended with a pledge to continue attempting to track the dark magic user, along with Jackson's promise to keep them informed. A frisson of guilt snaked through me. I shook it off. Telling them about me wouldn't help them track the dark magic user any better.

With the end of the meeting, Theresa, Evan, and Marcie said their goodbyes, but Matt approached Jackson. I started to join them, then noticed Jessica on the other side of the room. Now was my chance to talk with her alone.

"You wanted to speak with me." She spoke first. A statement, not a question. Interesting.

"Yes," I agreed with her non-question.

Jessica waited and when I did not continue, she did. "You're a witch."

"How did you know?"

"I can sense your magic."

Shock coursed through me. "What?"

"What kind of magic do you have?"

"You can sense my magic even though it's bound?" I answered a question with a question.

Her eyebrows furrowed in confusion. "Your magic is bound?"

"Yes."

She shook her head and peered closer at me. "It's muted, yes," she muttered. "Are you sure it's bound?"

"After my parents died—" Guilt flared and I stomped it down. "—I struggled with my magic. And, then—" Bile rose in my throat and I reversed direction. "—after another incident in college, I dropped out—"

Jessica shaking her head again stopped my rambling. "I don't know," she said, with a frown.

"I need your help," I said. "Five years ago, I signed a pact with Barbara Knollman to be her minion. I'd like to break the pact and unbind my powers."

Jessica frowned at the latter half of my request but responded to the former. "Let me do some research into breaking pacts with a low-level demon like her and I'll get back to you."

"Thank you so much," I responded, the tension radiating through my shoulders dropping a notch. Someone familiar with the demon was on the case! It was only a matter of time.

"What are you ladies talking about so intently?" Jackson's voice reached us before he did and our mouths snapped shut.

I gave a small shake of my head at Jessica, praying she would understand what I meant. "Just talking about magic," I answered.

Jackson glanced between us. "I can come back if you're not finished yet," he offered, uncertain.

"Nope, we're finished," I assured him and turned to Jessica. "It was great meeting you."

She leaned in for a goodbye hug, her mouth an inch from my ear. "Be careful," she whispered.

# CHAPTER TWELVE

I bit back my disappointment that the Witches Council hadn't been more helpful and focused on the group around me. We were at *Soprannaturale*, this time Jackson included. He had just finished filling in the ladies on what we learned. What little we had learned.

"Too bad they didn't know more," Catherine spoke first, giving voice to my own thoughts.

"At least we confirmed what we suspected – that there's somebody in town up to no good," Jackson countered. "If only we had a better idea of their goal." He frowned and three pairs of eyes bored into me. Oops. I guess they were expecting me to tell him why he was a target.

I sighed and Jackson looked at me. "Um." The waitress chose that moment to check on us. I accepted the reprieve and thought about how to explain that I withheld information from him.

The waitress walked away and all eyes returned to me.

"Did you learn something, Robin?"

Jackson's innocent question broke the dam and burning tears filled my eyes. "You were right about being the target. And you were right about me being the target," I said.

"I don't understand."

I haltingly explained Barbara wanting him dead for an unknown reason, my refusal to do so, and how she added me to the hit list. Jackson interrupted my spiel.

"Why would she ask you to kill me?"

The ladies exchanged glances before pointedly looking at me. I sidestepped. "I've been her gopher for five years. She's never asked something like that of me. I have no idea why she did now." I waited to see if the women would contradict me, or out me. Thankfully they didn't.

Jackson, however, still looked lost even with my explanation. No surprise there. It made little sense without the important fact of my minion status. I just couldn't bring myself to say that to him.

"Of course, now she believes I **am** going to kill you," I quipped.

Jackson's jaw dropped with my statement, so I took the edge off with a crooked grin.

"Misdirection, Jackson. I promise."

He laughed uneasily.

"We had hoped that if I told her I was back in line, that she would call off the replacement killer."

Understanding dawned in Jackson's eyes. "That makes more sense. Did it work?"

"No. She turned it into a game for her amusement," I finished bitterly. "Whoever kills you first – and the replacement killer still has me in his or her sights as well."

"That is unfortunate," he agreed. "At least that explains one thing."

"What?" Mia asked.

"Why my magic is drawn to protect Robin. It somehow sensed we were both targets that night. That's good. She'll have to stay with me for the next couple of days until this is over," Jackson insisted.

Warmth flooded me. I had no objection to staying by his side. "That sounds fine."

Catherine smothered a chuckle and I ignored the twinkle in her eye.

"What do we do now?" Evie bluntly asked. "If the Witches Council has no ideas…"

My disappointment surged again. Not only because of the reminder of their lack of knowledge of the black magic user, but because I didn't get to finish my conversation with Jessica afterward. The witch's confusion about my magic status perplexed me.

Was it possible that because I'd hidden it for years and then had it bound for years that it was distorted? That terrified me. What if my magic malfunctioned once we stopped Barbara and unbound it? I bounced my leg as I considered the alternatives. On the other hand, maybe the magic couldn't be read correctly while bound and it'd be fine after? Man, I hoped so. I'd have to be patient until Jessica did her research into breaking the pact with Barbara.

"Earth to Robin." Catherine waved a hand in front of my face and I blinked.

"Sorry, I was thinking."

"That much was obvious," Evie laughed.

"What's our next step?" I looked around the table after asking the question.

"I'm working on set tomorrow and I want Robin glued to my side."

I bit my lower lip at Jackson's statement and Mia grinned. I might be a great liar generally, but I sure wasn't hiding my… affection… for Jackson very well.

"That's a good idea from more than a protection standpoint," Catherine concurred. "Since both of you are targets, this gives the replacement killer something to target. When the killer makes his or her move, hopefully we'll get more information on their identity. And, more importantly, how to stop them."

Blood drained from my face. Awesome, let's make us targets. Or to be more accurate, we were officially bait.

# CHAPTER THIRTEEN

"I really don't think it's necessary to stay at your house," I argued with Jackson. He had followed me back to my home and we were standing in the kitchen.

"I thought you agreed you'd stay with me."

Oh, but I wanted to! "During the day, when we're out and about," I said instead, continuing to argue, but with little insistence.

"I'd stay here," he offered, "but we'd have to go get my equipment from my house for the shoot tomorrow. Plus, Buster would have to stay here too."

"Buster?"

"Didn't I mention him? He's my pittie mix."

"No, you didn't. I love dogs!"

"See," he said with an arched eyebrow, "it's just more logical to stay at my place. Wouldn't you feel bad if we left poor Buster on his own?"

I rolled my eyes. He had to know logic wasn't the issue. The thought of staying at Jackson's home… what would be the sleeping arrangements?

As though reading my mind, he wolfishly smiled. "I have a guest bedroom, if that's the concern."

I flushed and rocked back on my heels. "Um. Cool," I stammered. "That's good."

Jackson brushed his knuckles against my jawline, sending waves of pleasure through me. "If anything happened to you overnight, I'd never forgive myself."

The desire in his eyes brought my confusion to the surface. This couldn't be his protection magic. Could it?

"Pack for tonight and tomorrow. Please."

I melted a little at his tone, hearing the genuine worry underneath. "Okay," I relented. "Let me throw stuff in a bag and we can get going."

"Excellent! This'll be fun. Like a sleepover."

I choked on a laugh. "A sleepover?"

"Got you to laugh, didn't it?"

We smiled goofily at each other. My smile dropped. "Thanks."

"For what?"

"For just being there. For being you."

"I'm glad I could be. For you."

I couldn't believe we'd only met two days ago. I squeezed his upper arm, distracted for a moment by the rock-hard muscle underneath. Focus! "Give me a sec."

I dashed into the bedroom and flung open my closet door. I pulled out two long-sleeve t-shirts, another pair of jeans, and some undergarments. Sexy or plain? The question flashed in my mind. I shook my head and selected cotton undies. This wasn't a romantic getaway. He was protecting me from a demon who wanted us dead. I needed to remember that. My hand grabbed an extra set of lacy underthings. You know, just in case. I rolled my eyes at myself.

After grabbing toiletries from the bathroom, I stood again before Jackson. "Ready," I announced needlessly.

He reached to slide the overnight bag off my arm. "I've got this."

"Such a gentleman, thank you," I murmured.

He winked in reply.

I checked out his delicious backside for a moment before locking up my house and turning to follow him.

He stowed my bag behind the front passenger seat and fired up the truck. I saw his continual scanning for danger as he backed out of the driveway and began the short drive to his home.

"When did you realize you were a witch? Or should I be quiet so you can concentrate? You know, on sensing the danger."

Jackson chuckled. "Now that I'm on alert, I can sense energy changes just fine while we chat." He fiddled with the heater, and I wondered if he didn't want to talk about his paranormal history. "My parents knew I was a witch before I did."

"Wow, really? How?"

"My father is a witch, and the abilities pass on the father's side in my family, so he knew what to watch for. There are signs."

Would things have been different if I'd had that? I refused to start down that path, so I refocused on Jackson. "What kind of signs?"

"Mostly he watched for energy changes around me. Just like I can sense energy changes that signal the presence of magic, so can my Dad. He trained me to control my magic once it manifested at puberty."

"That's so cool." And I genuinely felt that way, though the roiling in my stomach confirmed some mixed feelings. "Where are your parents now?"

"They are traveling the world and very happy."

I could hear the smile in his voice as I stared out the windshield. How I wished I could have had that. Neither of my parents had been witches; they didn't know to watch for what had been happening to me.

"Everything okay?" Jackson asked.

"Why wouldn't it be?"

"Something seems off."

"Do you sense energy changes like before? Is this killer nearby?" We were passing the flashing sign announcing the sprawling Red Rock Casino complex headed toward the overpass for the 215 West Beltway. There were a fair number of cars, and lots of people in the buildings. Could he sense something from that distance? Or was he sensing my bound magic?

My peripheral vision caught his slight frown. "Not exactly."

"Not exactly?"

"It's not an exact science," he explained, and I heard the smile again in his voice, breaking the tension.

"My parents died just after my sixteenth birthday," I blurted out.

"Oh, Robin, I'm so sorry. That must have been tough," Jackson responded, reaching over to place his hand on my knee.

"It was. They died in a car accident. I was in foster care until I turned eighteen and aged out of the system." I glanced at Jackson. Relief flooded me when I saw sadness and not pity in his eyes. I hated people pitying me.

"When I talk about my happy life with my parents, that hurts," he surmised, surprising me.

"That sounds horrible when I hear it out loud, but yeah," I admitted.

"It's not horrible," he disagreed. "You're just being honest."

I shrugged. "Hmm." I feigned nonchalance, but my emotions churned. Jackson was attractive, thoughtful, sweet… perfect. I sighed.

"What's the sigh for?"

"You are entirely too perceptive and frank," I answered with a laugh, sidestepping the question.

Jackson echoed my laughter and turned the truck off of West Charleston Blvd onto a side street. I missed the sign, so didn't know quite where we were, but even in the dark, I could see this was one of the newer communities of cookie-cutter homes.

"I know they all look the same," Jackson said while maneuvering around a bend.

"You need to stop doing that."

"Doing what?"

"Reading my mind."

He grinned. "I don't have to read your mind. Many people have commented on the sameness of the beige stucco houses so close together." He parked in the driveway of a two-story version of precisely that. "And, yes, I can touch my wall and my neighbor's with just my arms outstretched."

I laughed.

"But that misses why people live out here," he continued.

"Why?"

"Easy access to Red Rock Canyon."

We opened our doors and exited the truck. "I could see how that would be a plus," I conceded. I pulled my bag from behind the seat and slammed the door closed.

Jackson slid my bag back off my shoulder like before. "I got that," he said and headed toward his door.

No point in arguing, so I followed him, noting the typical desert landscaping. "Nice cactus," I commented. He looked over his shoulder and I pointed to the massive cactus in the middle of his tiny yard. "It's taller than me."

"Indeed, it is. Beautiful flowers bloom on there, sometimes."

I turned my back to Jackson while he unlocked his door. All the houses around his were dark. Was everybody out or already asleep?

"Welcome to my humble abode," Jackson warmly welcomed me. The sound of claws on tile reached me and a muscular black dog flew across the room to greet me and his master. I crouched to accept the slobbery kisses. Jackson flipped the overhead lights on as I stood. While I took in the space, he rubbed the exposed belly of Buster, who had flopped over in front of him. I grinned before checking out the open floor plan that allowed me to see his living room, dining area, and kitchen all in one swoop. Pretty standard furniture. One feature stood out.

"Those posters are amazing."

"They are my favorite possessions; well, besides my camera equipment."

I walked the perimeter of his first floor, stopping to consider each framed movie poster. Many of them were even signed! I stopped in front of one and chuckled.

Jackson stood beside me. His warmth heated that side of my body.

"Not the best movie ever made," he agreed with my silent appraisal, "but *Sleepwalkers* is a classic bad movie by a master writer."

"Stephen King has contributed some of the worst films to celluloid, no doubt." I peered closer at the poster. "But, that's not his signature."

"Nope. Funny story. I was buying that poster at the San Diego Comic Con years ago—" He gave me the side-eye. "—yes, I go to Comic Cons."

I held up my hands with a laugh. "No judgment here. I love conventions," I enthused. "So, you were buying the poster—" I prompted.

"I was buying the poster and this guy standing next to me says, hey, I was on that set."

"No way!"

"Way!" We smiled at each other. "I asked him all about it and it turned out he was one of the camera guys. Of course, I asked him to sign the poster."

"Of course."

We continued to circle the room, ending up in the kitchen, which was nicely updated with stainless steel appliances and charcoal quartz countertops. Posh and manly. "Would you like a drink?"

"Water would be great. Since you bought this house to be close to Red Rock Canyon, how often do you hike?"

"Nearly every day I'm not working," he answered, his back to me while he poured a glass of water from a Brita pitcher. "Buster loves it." Hearing his name, the pup jumped from the couch and joined us in the kitchen area.

"He's adorable."

"And doesn't he know it." He leaned down to scratch Buster's head.

"Was he a rescue?"

"Not quite."

I raised an eyebrow.

"He's my familiar." Jackson took a sip of water, making eye contact over the top of the glass. "Do you know what that is?"

"I do. They're a witch's companion animal."

"Yep. He showed up when I hit puberty. And he'll be with me for as long as I'm a witch."

"I thought they were always cats," I joked, to cover the sudden tightness in my chest.

"Nope, not always cats."

"I had a cat as a child," I blurted impulsively. "Patches ran away after my parents' accident."

"I'm sorry, Robin." He reached for my hand.

My gaze dropped to his hand on mine. If a witch loses her familiar when she's no longer a witch… I pulled my hand free to grasp my glass, and raised my head.

"I've always wanted to adopt another one. The timing never seemed right." College student on campus.

Homeless. Demon's minion. Yeah, the timing had never been right. I snorted.

"What's that about?"

I shook my head. "Nothing. But one day I plan to adopt a cat."

"We'll have to do a playdate once you adopt," Jackson joked.

I quirked an eyebrow. "We will?"

"We'll want to make sure our animals get along, right?"

"Um. Yes?"

Jackson laughed his low and sexy laugh. "I'm just teasing you, Robin. You turn a delightful shade of red when you're embarrassed."

A flush crept up my neck. "Gee, thanks."

Jackson came around the island and engulfed me in a bear hug.

I held my breath a moment before relaxing into his embrace. He smelled nice, clean. I rested my head on his chest.

"Everything will be okay."

"You promise?" My voice trembled with the question.

"If I have anything to say about it, I will do everything in my power to protect you."

Protect me. Yeah. I disengaged from the hug and stared up at him. "We should go to bed."

My flush deepened when he waggled his eyebrows at me. I pushed against his solid wall of a chest.

"You know what I mean," I protested.

Jackson leaned in and whispered in my ear. "Yes, I do."

I closed my eyes briefly at the wave of anticipation before taking a step back. "You have work in the morning," I reminded him.

"Follow me," he responded with another chuckle, grabbing my overnight bag off the couch. We walked up a flight of carpeted stairs and down a short tiled hallway.

"This is the guest bedroom." A queen-size bed and a single chest of drawers, all in a deep cherry wood, filled the space.

"It looks lovely, thanks."

"There's an attached bathroom, and I'll be just down the hall if you need anything."

I swallowed. "Um, okay."

Jackson twirled a strand of my hair in his fingers. "Don't hesitate to ask."

I folded my hand over his. "I won't."

Pleasure thrummed through me until he pulled back. "I won't let anyone hurt you."

Right. The protection magic. "Goodnight, Jackson."

He stepped out of the room, pausing in the doorway. "Goodnight, Robin. I'll wake you up at 8, okay?"

"Sounds good."

He closed the door soundlessly behind him. Carpet muffled his steps as he walked to his bedroom down the hall. I swallowed again.

I unpacked my few belongings and got cleaned up in the bathroom. Snuggling under the down comforter, perfect for Vegas in December, I sighed.

Was Jackson sending mixed signals or was I misreading? Protection magic was very confusing.

# CHAPTER FOURTEEN

Jackson's guest bedroom mattress begged me to stay in it, so I snuggled further under the covers. I thought I heard movement downstairs and sighed. It must be time to get up. The sound drew closer and I smiled when I recognized claws on tile. Soon, an 80-pound dog jumped onto the bed and gave me morning kisses.

"Hey, Buster, good morning to you, too." I scratched him behind his ear and was rewarded with a thumping leg against the bed. "You like that, don't you, big guy?" Buster's head rose and he sniffed the air. A second later, I too smelled the scent of bacon wafting up the stairs. Mmm, was Jackson making breakfast?

I looked down at my pajamas, debating whether to change. Friends don't have to get cleaned up for breakfast, I decided, and headed downstairs toward the delicious smells.

"Good morning, sunshine," Jackson greeted me with a smile.

A hand went to my hair; how bad was my bed head this morning?

He chuckled. "You look fine. Like you just woke up. Did Buster wake you?"

"Yes, but it's not a bad way to start the day."

"Hungry?"

"Very." I approached him, standing in front of the stove. "That looks yummy."

He flipped the omelet with a spatula in one hand and the bacon with a second spatula in the other.

"Impressive."

"I got skills."

"Indeed." My heart sped up at the double entendre in our exchange.

"How did you sleep?"

"Like the dead," I responded before wincing. Maybe not the best analogy when people were trying to kill you.

Jackson belly-laughed. "Perfect." He pointed toward an overhead cupboard to my right. "If you want to grab a couple of plates—" He pointed to a drawer below. "—and silverware, breakfast will be ready in a few minutes."

"How did you time this so perfectly?" I asked, marveling at the coordination.

He grinned. "I didn't. I planned to wake you up if Buster or the smell didn't," he admitted and I laughed.

"That would have worked, too."

After serving up the food, we sat at his dining room table to eat, Buster splayed on the floor, watching hopefully for a piece of bacon to drop.

"This is beautiful," I expressed, running my fingers over the light-ash distressed wood.

"Thank you," he murmured, though I didn't miss how his eyes watched my hand move along the top of the table.

I snatched my hand back and his lips quivered like he was biting back a smile. "What's the plan for today?"

"We were going to be filming in the Bellagio atrium," he started.

"The botanical gardens, where they decorate for the season?" I interrupted. "I love seeing what they've done with the flowers!"

"Unfortunately," he continued, with another smile at my enthusiasm, "production made a last-minute change and now we're shooting at a house in North Las Vegas. I've got the address on my phone."

"Too bad." We ate in silence for a few moments. "I'm looking forward to watching you work."

"I would think with your experience in the industry, it'd be boring by now," he teased.

I flushed and lifted a single shoulder. "It's not." Besides, my traitorous mind added, I planned to enjoy the scenery.

Jackson eyed my empty plate. "I'll clear the table if you want to get ready. We need to leave in fifteen minutes."

"Aye, aye, sir," I responded with a salute. His laughter followed me back up the stairs.

*****

I was right. I was enjoying the view. We'd arrived at the house for filming and after making sure I had everything I needed – sweetly protective, was my Jackson – he got to work. The morning passed in a blur of filming. We were approaching our late afternoon lunch time when I saw Jackson freeze. The hair on the back of my neck rose and I scanned the rooms I could see. The living room was empty, save for the owner's sage green couch and ottoman. Production staff milled around the white dining room table covered end to end with scripts, backpacks, and coffee containers. Lights were being set in the large, country-style kitchen, presumably because that was where the next scene would be shot. Nothing appeared out of the ordinary.

Jackson set his camera equipment on the floor and stood ramrod straight. His gaze found me and I saw the stark fear in his eyes.

"Get out now!" Jackson startled everyone with his unexpected yell. Silence fell over the room. He was already moving toward me. "Get out now!" he repeated, grabbing my arm and pulling me toward the front door. I heard movement behind me, along with shouts and confused questions.

Jackson flung the door open and lifted me through the frame. A crush of bodies followed us. An awful cracking filled the air. I turned to identify the noise. Jackson tackled me to the ground. I landed on the dirt with a thump, thanking the homeowners for not putting in desert rock landscaping. The cracking built until reaching a crescendo. The roof collapsed into itself, dust rising as it fell. My fingers tingled and energy raced along my arms. My eyes cut to the front door, where another person darted out, rubbing his face. A wild glance around the front yard showed nine people outside the building. My eyes settled on Jackson, still clutching me, his body sheltering me from the imploding home, an unreadable expression now on his face.

"Do you feel that?" he asked.

"Feel what?" I sank into his body, heart rate slowing, breathing evening out, and that weird tingling subsiding. He shook his head and held me closer. "Is that everybody?" I asked breathlessly.

The silence that followed was absolute. Nobody spoke. No birds chirped. No cars drove past.

"Are you okay?" Jackson asked, his hands skimming over me, checking for injuries. Normally I would have enjoyed this closeness, but horror held me.

"I'm fine. Did everybody make it out?" I repeated.

Jackson jumped to his feet. His face paled as he made the same count I did. He ran toward the devastated home.

"Jackson!" I yelled after him, terrified the building wasn't safe. I continued to stare after he vanished from sight. Time stood still while I waited. Voices filtered through my haze as the cast and crew checked in with each other. I thought I heard someone calling 9-1-1. My eyes remained fixed on the door.

Jackson appeared. He carried a woman in his arms. At first, I thought she wasn't moving. Then her torso shook with a cough. Thank goodness! Jackson gave me a wan smile when he met my gaze and I clutched my arms tight. I sent positive thoughts into the universe that she'd be okay.

Time resumed normal speed for me. I stood, shaking from the adrenaline dump. The police arrived. An ambulance arrived and took the woman in Jackson's arms away. EMTs checked everybody over. I received only a cursory glance, which was fine. I was fine.

But what had happened?

# CHAPTER FIFTEEN

Jackson and I sat in his truck. A blanket wrapped around me kept my shivering to a minimum. But I wasn't shivering from the cold.

"What happened?" I asked, fearing I already knew the answer.

"Someone tried to kill us."

I took a deep, shaky breath. "That's what I thought. What happened?" I asked again.

"Whoever's using the black magic caved in the roof."

I nodded, unable to speak now that my fears had been confirmed.

Jackson's face hardened. "And this time, he or she nearly killed someone. Almost killed Jane."

"This is my fault," I whispered.

Jackson clasped my hands in his. "No, Robin, it's not. It's whoever is using this magic."

I shook my head, unwilling to accept his absolution. "Yes, it is. If I hadn't been working for Barbara, none of this would have happened."

Jackson thumbed a single tear off my cheek. "Yes, it would have. Barbara is out to kill me. You were just supposed to be the one to do it," Jackson reminded me.

"That's true, I suppose," I agreed with a watery smile. "But it was my decision to draw out the hired killer," I reminded him.

"No," he contradicted. "It was a group decision. This is not your fault," he repeated.

"Agree to disagree?"

"No. But, I'll agree to table the discussion for another time," he offered with a half-smile.

I closed my eyes briefly, offered a tired smile of my own in return. "You saved me again."

"Yes. And I will every time."

"We need this to end."

"It will. In two days, right?"

I nodded. The demon's one-week demand would end in two days. This would be over, one way or the other. How many people might die before then? I mentally slapped myself. I couldn't think like that, couldn't allow the possibility of more blood on my hands. A solution would be found. We just needed to be proactive.

"We need to meet with the ladies, talk about next steps." I forced out the next words. "Our choice to be bait almost got someone killed." I held up a hand to stop him from disagreeing. "I can't be responsible for that again. We need to take control."

"Okay. Plan a meeting for tonight." Jackson pulled me into his arms and breathed into my hair. "I promise nothing will happen to you."

I nodded against his shoulder. "Your protection magic won't let it."

A moment passed before he responded. "That's right. It won't."

And I made my own promise. To myself. Nobody would die. And, even if I was wrong that Jackson's interest in me was more than his protection magic, maybe I could convince him that our attraction was real.

CHAPTER SIXTEEN

I couldn't believe only two hours had passed since the roof caved in on set. This time we met in a more private location, Mia's house in The Lakes. A quick ten-minute drive up West Desert Inn Road had brought me to her waterfront home.

Now, I sat on Mia's turquoise couch (I guess as a mermaid – sorry, nixie – she really loved the water!) and surveyed the gathered group. Besides me, Mia, Jackson, Catherine, and Evie, Mia's boyfriend, homicide detective Jacob Dawson, was also present. That threw me for a moment. Did Jackson's co-worker Jane die? Dread increased as I waited for someone to speak.

"Is Jane okay?" I blurted out, unable to stand waiting any longer.

Jacob understood my question. "Yes, she is. She woke up on the way to the hospital and they're keeping her overnight for observation, but they expect her to make a full recovery."

I breathed a sigh of relief. Jackson reached over to squeeze my hand. Catherine caught the movement and smiled knowingly. A blush bloomed across my face. Sheesh.

"And before you ask," Jacob continued. "I'm here because of my involvement in the last major entertainment related attacks."

Mia laughed, the sound like tinkling bells. Everyone turned to her.

Jacob rolled his eyes.

"Tell them your new nickname, Jacob," she demanded playfully.

"I'd rather not."

"Please, tell us," Catherine insisted.

Jacob shook his head. "Detective Hollywood," he mumbled.

Evie belly laughed. "That's fantastic!"

Tension in the room dropped with this ice breaker and after teasing Jacob for a few more moments, we got down to business.

"Thank you all again for your help," Jackson began. "Robin and I know it wasn't easy for you to help her, given your history with Barbara."

"We don't want anyone using black magic in Vegas," Mia said. "This is much bigger than Barbara and Robin."

"True," Jackson agreed. "Let's start with what we know, to bring Jacob up to speed."

"Robin's demon boss ordered her to kill you," Evie jumped in with a wink at me.

"Evie," Catherine admonished the vampire. "Robin said no."

Evie shrugged, but a twinkle remained in her eye. Was she teasing me?

"A new killer was hired," Catherine continued, "with Robin added to the hit list. We had Robin pretend to be back on board."

I picked up the story. "This unfortunately backfired, and if the killer sticks to Barbara's original timetable, he or she has two days left to kill the two of us."

Catherine looked at us, worry etched on her face. "We have that same amount of time, therefore, to find and stop this killer."

And find a way to break my pact with Barbara and unbind my powers, I silently added. Catherine's expression told me she was having the same additional thought.

"And this killer has now tried to kill you both twice?" Jacob asked.

Jackson and I nodded.

"And you've been able to sense the magic being used by this person?"

"Yes," Jackson answered Jacob's follow-up question.

"But nobody has any idea who the new killer is?"

"I checked in with the Family," Evie answered the detective's question. "They said the hired killer isn't known to them."

We considered this declaration. The vampire Family in Las Vegas sometimes used Cleaners who would take out (okay, kill) humans, vampires, or other beings that were a threat to the Family. Taking the Family's response at face value, that meant our replacement killer was unlikely to be a vampire.

"And I checked in with Alex," Catherine added. "He said he's not aware of any nonhuman supernatural being in town who's been hired for a contract killing, nor have his contacts heard any rumblings." If her half-incubus boyfriend, who had an in with most of the supernatural underworld, said the hired killer wasn't a nonhuman supernatural being, that was probably accurate.

"What does that leave us?" I asked.

"A human witch, as I suspected," Jackson answered with a scowl.

"Using you guys as bait turned out to be too dangerous," Mia said. "Does anybody have any ideas about what we can do next? Jacob?"

"Using the media to draw out the last killer worked," he answered. Mia blanched. He took her hand, and she smiled at the offered comfort. From what I understood, it had hit her hard earlier this year, when she killed a djinn in self-defense to protect Jacob.

"How can we do something like that with Liz this time?" Catherine asked.

Elizabeth Addison, co-host of the popular morning show, *Entertainment Daily*, had directly challenged the djinn on her show to lure her out. It had worked and the killing was stopped. Of course, her expose outing the supernatural underworld shortly followed. As far as I knew, nobody liked her anymore.

"Is she still doing that ridiculous *Mythical Being of the Week* segment on the show?" Catherine rolled her eyes.

"Unfortunately, yes. I believe it's the highest rated story every time," Mia answered with a crooked smile.

"I never should have confirmed our existence for her," Evie groused and my eyebrows raised.

"Evie gave Liz an exclusive on the paranormal underworld in exchange for her vouching for Mia when Jacob thought she was in cahoots with the djinn," Catherine explained. "None of this is your fault, Evie."

"I know that," she retorted. "It still just galls me."

"Would Elizabeth even help us?" I asked.

Mia shrugged. "Liz would if there was something in it for her."

Ah, another shining example of the self-interested media. Who was I kidding? A demon's minion judging a reporter? That was pretty cheeky.

"I have an idea," I spoke slowly, the pieces falling into place in my head. When I finished presenting the stages of my plan to the others, slow nods surrounded me. A few suggested tweaks and we were ready. Time to implement Stage One (and yes, I capitalized it; it was our grand plan, after all!).

# CHAPTER SEVENTEEN

Jackson and I arrived back at his place well after nightfall. Darkness shrouded his neighbors' homes. He parked the car and we hurried inside. Buster nosed Jackson's hand, whimpering.

"It's okay. We have a plan," Jackson assured his familiar.

The dog chuffed and sat on his haunches, waiting to see what we would do. The first step in our plan was all Jackson. He would create his force field around the house.

"Ready to see the magic happen?"

I clapped like an excited schoolgirl. "You know it."

He walked to one corner of the home. "This is essentially true north," he began. "I'll bring forth my magic—"

"How?" I interrupted. Buster chuffed again, and I swore he was laughing at my question.

Jackson shrugged. "It's not an exact science. I concentrate on the feeling of magic in my core and focus it on this corner. I'll do the same in the other directions."

"Directions?"

"Compass directions. The closest spots in the house to true north, west, east, and south."

I nodded. I vaguely remembered about the importance of the Earth's compass when I first started researching Wicca after my parents' deaths. Jackson didn't buy my feigned understanding.

"In Earth magic, we call to the power of nature."

"Even when it's within you?"

"Yep. Witches draw their strength from Mother Earth, no matter what their specific brand of magic is."

"Okay, that makes sense."

Jackson closed his eyes and reached a hand toward the corner. I waited for him to start a spell or something. He opened his eyes. "Done."

"Wait. That's it? What about a spell? Or incantation?" Even as I asked the questions, I remembered my brief use of magic years ago; I certainly hadn't used any spells. Jackson confirmed what I just concluded.

"It's internal, mostly. Group magic uses spells, but otherwise, it's often inside the witch."

Buster and I followed Jackson as he moved to each of the directional spots and repeated the same silent magic.

"How will it stay active?"

"Since I won't be able to maintain my focus on it to keep it at full strength, it's like a thin layer of force field. Like icing on a cake."

"Very cool."

"All finished. This will somewhat hide us from tracking magic."

"Somewhat?"

"If someone's motivated enough—"

"You mean, like someone who wants us dead?" I quipped.

Jackson chuckled. "Yes, I suppose." His smile dropped. "If someone's motivated enough, they could find us. But, if the killer doesn't know to search deeper, he or she probably won't be able to."

"Probably?" I squeaked.

"The force field would also protect against initial magic attacks. Any attack on my magic would wake me up, and then allow me to focus on the force field to reinforce it."

"That sounds better."

"Bottom line, it's unlikely anyone would bother to attack us here, even if they found us," he reassured me.

"That's good." A big yawn threatened to crack my face in half.

"Looks like it's time for bed."

At the final word, my face flushed and his eyes dilated. I yawned again and the moment was broken. Exhaustion had caught up with me. With a little wave, I scurried from the living room. Buster yelped a goodnight. And was that rumbly noise Jackson laughing? Pssht. Goofball. I changed into my pajamas and fell into a deep sleep the instant my head hit the pillow in Jackson's guest room.

# CHAPTER EIGHTEEN

Stage One had the potential to be boring. Luckily it wasn't. Our part of the plan for day six of the Killer Countdown, as I had taken to calling it (joking kept the anxiety at bay... right?), was to stay out of sight. The plan called for us not to be targets until exactly the right moment. That meant we hid out in Jackson's place for the day, beneath his protection force field.

But others were more active.

I knew Mia and Elizabeth Addison had worked together to stop a murderous djinn earlier in the year and thought they had had a falling out. Turned out I was right. Also turned out that Mia was right. As soon as she offered Liz exclusivity in reporting our full story when it concluded, Liz was on board.

Thus, that morning, Jackson and I sat with Buster on the couch waiting for Liz to set our plan into motion.

"Good morning in the Valley!" Liz Addison welcomed viewers to her show, *Entertainment Daily*, her wide, toothy smile in place. "Some of you may have seen the *Forbidden Island* movie production filming scenes around town. If you've ever wanted to be on a movie set," she enticed viewers, "now's your chance. Producers have informed us that they are looking for background talent – that's extras to you and me – for a big scene tonight."

At first, we worried this would be too risky. What would happen if a bunch of people showed up to a fake set? After all, this was a lure. We didn't want anybody showing up. But then we realized, it was easily handled…

"If that's you," Liz pointed a perfectly manicured hand at the camera, "then head to our website, click on the link, and email the production your interest. They'll send the location to the first people to reply. Spots are limited," she warned viewers. What nobody watching (except us, of course) knew was that when they clicked on the link, they'd be sadly informed that all the spots for the evening's filming were filled. Too bad, so sad. But exactly according to our plan. Liz turned to face another camera, her short, curly brown hair gently swinging. "Interested in animal welfare," she began, and Jackson pressed the mute button.

"And there it is. Our invitation to the replacement killer to come and get us," Jackson said quietly.

At the word killer, my heart rate jumped erratically. "Do you think it'll work?"

"It was your plan," he reminded me. "Don't you think it will work?"

I did. The replacement killer knew Jackson and I were together, and that Jackson was working the movie. We hoped that after frustrating the replacement killer all day by hiding out, he or she would jump at the chance to nail us on set.

"One potential flaw in setting up the plan is if the replacement killer doesn't hear about filming tonight," I voiced my concern.

"Didn't Mia say Liz promised to blast the background actor invitation all over social media once the show wrapped?"

"She did." My bouncing leg slowed.

"Wouldn't that then practically guarantee the replacement killer would hear about the filming tonight?"

"Yes, it would." I took a deep breath. "I'm also still concerned about the killer knowing where we'll be."

"Weren't you also the one that said when the replacement killer knows there's filming but not the location, he or she would just wait for us to leave? And then follow us?"

I tilted my head back, contemplating the ceiling. "Yes. I said those things too."

"Then aren't we okay?"

"Yes, we are." I met his gaze. "Thank you. I needed that."

"You're welcome." Jackson took a sip of his coffee. "Tonight's the final night before Barbara's deadline, and possibly the last chance for the replacement killer to strike. He or she will wait for us to leave and follow us to set. It'll work."

I nodded. "Yes." It had to.

*****

When *Entertainment Daily* concluded, Liz was true to her word. Jackson and I popped on our laptops to confirm that word of the filming was all over social media. Now the waiting would begin. We didn't plan to arrive on set until just after the sun set around 5 p.m. That left about six hours to kill, I mean, to wait.

"What do you want to do while we wait?"

Jackson asked the question innocently, but man did my body respond not-so-innocently. "Play a board game?" I responded.

He gave me a knowing smile but didn't comment. "Let me show you what I have."

I'd like to see what you have, my traitorous mind whispered. I ignored it and followed him to a hutch in the dining area filled with board games. That successfully distracted me.

"These are all the games I have. Are any of these speaking to you?"

"How about *Ticket to Ride Europe*?" I'd never played the game, but it looked interesting.

"Great choice," Jackson enthused. "It's a strategy game where the person who builds the most railway wins." He pulled the game out of the hutch and we set up on the kitchen table, Buster in his primary location at our feet.

And thus, the day went by… playing games, chit chatting, watching the noon news. Butterflies took flight in my stomach as the declining sun through the window blinds informed me it was almost time. By that point, we were back sitting on the couch, watching one of those judge shows on television.

"How are you feeling?" Jackson asked, taking one of my hands in his.

I squeezed his fingers. "Nervous," I admitted.

"I'd be worried if you weren't."

"Are you?"

"Nervous? Yes. I would hate if something happened to you." He rubbed my fingers, the sensations sending warmth through my body.

"Same here," I said thickly.

"You would hate if something happened to you?" he asked.

A glance in his direction showed him smirking. "Yes, I would," I responded with a wink. "But I'd also hate if something happened to you."

"It won't."

"You promise?"

"I do."

Feeling more secure, but still acutely aware of that swarm of butterflies in my belly, I stood. "It's time."

# CHAPTER NINETEEN

In order to have a fairly isolated set, we chose an abandoned house in Boulder City, about an hour from Jackson's house, just outside metro Las Vegas. This was our attempt to keep damage to a minimum, in case everything went sideways. We listened to the local classic rock station, 97.1 The Point, as we trekked across the city. The music wasn't quite the distraction I'd hoped for, but it kept my leg bouncing to a minimum.

We pulled into the driveway of a sprawling one-story home right on the edge of the desert. This definitely fit the bill for isolated! A handful of cars were already parked in the driveway and along the street.

Given the distance we had to drive, I assumed that meant we were the last to arrive. That was okay; it meant everybody would be more likely to be ready when the replacement killer struck. We couldn't block off the street, secluded though it was, and so Jacob positioned police at the homes on each end. We expected everything to go down fast. I doubted they'd have much of a chance to do anything. But they could act as an early warning system if any cars drove down the street.

Since we didn't know when the replacement killer would strike, we needed to pretend to film. Even so, my jaw dropped when Jackson pulled open the large wooden front door.

It looked like a genuine film set. Evie and Ryan, two of the actors in our group, stood in an empty living room holding sheets of paper. I idly wondered if they brought past scripts with them or if those were blank pages.

A standard three-point lighting set-up surrounded the actors. Someone had positioned the key light, or primary light, behind Evie and Ryan. I smothered a laugh; the dramatic lighting that position provided seemed fitting for this evening's activities. A fill light, to illuminate unwanted shadows, was positioned next to the camera, a nicer-than-expected Canon EOS C300 Mark II (though still only half the cost of a $20,000 RED 8K camera… but I digressed). And, finally, the backlight, an ARRI 150, I thought, was positioned behind and above the actors.

Catherine stood behind the camera, fiddling with it. Did she know anything about them or was she completely pretending?

I shook my head. It was so real – and yet so fake.

Mia and her homicide detective boyfriend, Jacob, stood off to the side of the tableau, pretending to refer to a clipboard of paper.

Alex, Catherine's half-incubus boyfriend, stood on the other side of the room. He was the only one that drew attention; he seemed to be standing guard, which he was.

"Hey, everyone. Are we ready to shoot this thing?" Jackson asked jovially.

A chorus of hellos returned the greeting. I saw worry reflected in several sets of eyes. We would have to pretend to film until Jackson sensed the energy change that heralded the replacement killer's arrival. And then we would have a small window to launch our offensive defense. I didn't know if that was a thing, but it fit what I felt we were doing. We set everything up but we would only respond when the replacement killer launched a volley, so to speak.

*****

Three hours later, we'd run out of fake filming to do and boredom had set in. I hoped this wouldn't be a bust. Then what would we do? The deadline was tomorrow. Who knew what Barbara would do if Jackson wasn't dead? I was on the fence over whether or not she'd care if I was dead.

Jacob pulled his phone from his pocket in response to a text notification. "Another car pulled onto the street," he informed us in a low voice. This was the third car in three hours. The first time we had gone on high alert. And nothing happened. The second time we had gone on high alert. And nothing happened. This time I felt the tension rise, but nobody moved. A fence surrounded the perimeter of the property and we'd locked all the doors to the house. We hoped this would corral our killer to the front, and keep him or her on the street.

Jacob continued to watch his phone. "The car parked one house over."

Alex rolled onto the balls of his feet. He clenched and unclenched his hands.

Minutes passed with no update.

"Car door is opening," Jacob murmured.

Evie and Ryan set their script pages on the floor. Evie faced the front door and Ryan faced the window to their side.

"Someone in a hooded cape has exited the car."

"How cliché," I muttered with an eye roll. Catherine half-snorted in response.

Everyone stood at alert.

"The individual has stopped in front of the house. Unable to tell if male or female. They remain in the street."

Jackson held his hands out in front of him like he was calling for an *amen* from the congregation.

We waited with bated breath.

"It's time!" Jackson flung the front door open.

# CHAPTER TWENTY

"You don't have to do this," Jackson implored the figure standing in the street. We formed a loose group behind Jackson at the front door. Watching. Waiting.

"Yes, I do," the figure responded. I felt the startled reactions around me. The voice was decidedly feminine. A female replacement killer. Why was I not surprised? Guess Barbara was into equal opportunity.

"No, you don't," Jackson disagreed. Tension rolled off of him, but his voice remained calm.

"I signed a contract. If I don't fulfill it, I don't get paid." The female witch raised her hands. "I intend to finish the job."

At those words, Jackson raced outside, the rest of us following behind. He stopped about twenty feet from the killer. Even in the dark, at this distance, I could see the woman's features. She appeared mid-twenties, her eyes weirdly lit. Oh, wait, they just reflected the light pouring from the open door of our fake set.

Jackson raised his arms in front of him to match hers. This was looking like a high noon duel. You know, if they happened at night between two witches. I shook my head at the crazy thought. Those anxious butterflies from before seemed caught in a maelstrom in my stomach.

"I've never not finished a contract," the female witch continued. "The two of you will end up dead before the sun rises." She dropped her hands for a moment. "And any of you who get in my way," she added.

"Her energy is building," Jackson yelled as the female witch raised her hands above her head. "Mia! You're up."

Mia stepped in front of Jackson, her green hair flowing down her back and lifting slightly in the breeze. "None of this is necessary, is it? Everyone can walk away tonight, unharmed." Her melodious magical voice washed over all of us.

She was right. There was no reason for any of this unpleasantness. The female witch lowered her arms. I breathed a sigh of relief that everything would be okay.

Mia faced us, breaking the spell. "Evie!"

I had a moment to remember that Mia had warned us that we would be bewitched along with the replacement killer.

And she couldn't do it for long because it could interfere with the rest of the plan.

The female witch immediately raised her hands. Several large boulders from the yard around us rose with them. Sweat beaded on my forehead.

Evie stepped forward. The female witch's arms ceased moving. The boulders hung suspended in the air. Evie did it! I wouldn't have believed it if I hadn't seen it for myself. The vampire stopped time. She excluded our small bubble of people of course. "Jacob, you're up."

Jacob took several steps toward the female witch. I hugged myself in delight. It was going to work! Jacob would get the cuffs on the female witch while she stood frozen in time. When he was still five feet away, the witch's hands trembled.

"She's breaking free! I can't hold all of this much longer! Time's going to restart!" Evie shouted. "Jacob, grab her quickly! Jackson, the force field!"

Each of Evie's shouts rocked me. No, no, no. This couldn't happen. The plan would work.

I reached out both hands, uncertain how I could help keep the plan from failing. My fingers began to tingle and energy raced along my skin. I shook my arms as though the pins and needles feeling was caused by them falling asleep. I didn't know what was happening, but something was building and itching for release.

A vague memory from my teenage years surfaced, and I knew.

I remembered what happened with my parents.

"Jacob, get back! I can handle this." I felt the eyes of the others on me. Time fully restarted and the female witch prepared to hurl the boulders at our group.

Energy crackled off of me, around me. My fingers lit up with blue electricity. The wind howled, almost like a cyclone. Distracted, the witch dropped the boulders and stared. I met her eyes and smiled grimly.

A lightning bolt sizzled out of the sky, striking the female witch. She crumpled to the ground. A scent of ozone permeated the air.

Jacob raced forward to check the unmoving witch's pulse. He looked back at the group and shook his head.

I dropped my hands in shock. The witch was dead. The immediate danger had passed. We would still need to handle Barbara. But a bigger question loomed. I knew it and as the eyes of the group fell upon me again, they knew it.

What had just happened? My magic was back. How was that possible?

A tentative hand touched my shoulder from behind. I sensed it was Jackson before he spoke. "Are you okay?" That one question held volumes of unasked questions. I turned to face him, to face the others.

"I think so," I whispered.

My phone trilled an incoming call. Out of habit, I answered. "Hi, Jessica," I greeted her, nary a tremor in my voice.

"What happened?" She echoed my earlier internal question. "We sensed a huge display of magic outside of town."

"It's over," I told her, a bone-deep weariness settling over me. "The replacement killer is dead."

"Come to the Council. Now," Jessica demanded.

I glanced around at Catherine, Evie, Ryan, Mia, Jacob, Alex, and Jackson. Looking for permission? I didn't even know. My mind swirled.

"Go. We'll take care of everything here," Catherine assured me, having heard Jessica's directive. Jacob nodded. If local law enforcement said it was okay… I guessed it was.

"Come with me?" I asked Jackson.

"Of course."

He propped me up, and I shuffled beside him to his truck. He helped me into the front passenger seat. A wave of exhaustion washed over me; maybe a quick cat nap during the drive would be okay.

# CHAPTER TWENTY-ONE

Warm breath in my ear woke me from my restless sleep. "We're here, Robin. Time to talk to Jessica and the Witches Council."

At the phrase, I bolted upright in the seat and trained wide eyes on Jackson. "I hope they have some answers."

"I'm sure they will," he responded while lifting me out of the truck and setting me gently on the ground. His face held an inscrutable expression.

There were lots of questions there, I knew. He supported me as we walked up the short sidewalk to the squat industrial building housing the Council chamber. Soon we stood before the five council members seated behind the half-circle table. I had trouble meeting their gazes. Instead, my eyes wandered over the silvery wallpaper reflecting the light from the antique wall sconces. I stood rigidly in front of my chair.

"You are a witch," Theresa began. A statement, not a question. She had replaced her red lipstick with bright purple today.

"Yes."

"Please tell us what happened in Boulder City," Matt, the older gentleman requested.

With only a few verbal stumbles, I relayed what had happened earlier that evening with the replacement killer. A few eyebrows rose when I revealed the witch was female, but otherwise, the Council remained silent until I finished.

"How were you able to summon the lightning bolt?" Marcie, the young woman who still struck me as barely out of her teens, but surely was older, asked the question. I heard genuine curiosity and wondered if Jessica had told the Council about my bound magic.

I glanced at Jackson. Now was a moment of truth. He knew I had hidden my witch status from him. Time to lay all my cards on the table, as they said. "I discovered I had abilities after puberty. I'm not sure what to call them, but I discovered I could—" I hesitated, uncertain how to describe my skills. "—control the weather? I guess that's the best way to explain it."

"Elemental powers, then?" Evan, the tall, heavyset witch asked.

"I suppose so. But my parents didn't understand what was happening any more than I did." My voice choked with the mention of my parents.

"They weren't witches?" Marcie appeared surprised.

"Not as far as I know." I swallowed. "I think they were afraid of me." Tears filled my eyes. "They should have been."

"What happened, Robin?" Jessica asked.

"When I was sixteen, we were driving to yet another appointment with a psychiatrist. Over the three years prior, they had taken me to doctor after doctor, who tried medication after medication." I winced at the bitterness in my voice.

"We were arguing. I remember being so angry at them. I couldn't understand why they couldn't understand how cool this was. I could control the weather. What teenager wouldn't want something like out of a comic book movie?" I smiled sadly.

"But everything came apart that day. We were yelling, and suddenly I felt my arms tingling from my shoulders to the tips of my fingers. I hadn't experienced it so strongly and didn't at first realize what was happening." I dropped my gaze to my fidgeting fingers.

"A bolt of lightning struck the car and we drove off the highway into a light pole. My parents died instantly," I finished in a rush of words. I heard pens on papers in the stillness following my admission.

I risked a glance at Jackson. My heart froze at his expressionless face. I returned my gaze to the Council. "I buried my magic deep after that, while I was in foster care.

After aging out of the program at eighteen, I attempted college." I stopped, unable to catch my breath.

"What happened during college?" Evan asked.

"My magic went on the fritz," I answered. "Lightning bolts, hurricane force winds. I lost control. So, I dropped out and lived on the street where I couldn't hurt anyone."

"How did you wind up in Vegas?" Marcie asked.

"I just drifted here," I said with a shrug. "But one day I had had enough. After four years on the street, I couldn't do it anymore and I begged the universe to help me." I rolled onto the balls of my feet. My final big reveal to Jackson. How his mind must be reeling. "Barbara Knollman answered my call."

The Council members stirred in their seats at my admission. Of course, they knew she was a demon. Everyone in the paranormal world knew that.

"I signed a pact with the demon to be her minion if she would help me. She created the circumstances for me to start my talent agency and bound my magic. Everything was stable, if not actually good, until she ordered me to kill Jackson McKee. And I refused."

Matt was frowning, bald head tilted up toward the ceiling. He refocused on me. "How did you release your magic?"

"I don't know. I was hoping you could answer that."

"I can," Jessica interjected. All eyes swiveled to her. "The demon never bound your magic, Robin."

My jaw dropped. "Yes, she did."

"No, she didn't."

"Then why couldn't I feel it anymore."

"You denied it for so long it became trapped within you."

"I did?"

"If I had to guess," Jessica continued, "I'd say guilt over your parents' deaths and the instability in college drove you to burying your powers."

A tear fell. "I bound my own powers?"

"In a manner of speaking, yes."

Evan shifted his bulk to sit forward in his seat. Kind eyes peered at me. "And then you could access it when your friends were in danger." The other Council members nodded.

"I could?"

"Yes, Robin, you could," Jessica answered.

Jackson spoke. "How does she break the pact with the demon?"

# CHAPTER TWENTY-TWO

Jackson settled his hand on my shoulder following his question. I took comfort in the touch while we waited for the Council to reply. I wasn't sure if Jessica had informed the other members about our conversation… had that only been two days ago? Time flies when you're having fun. Not.

"That's a good question, Jackson," Jessica responded. "I did some research after Robin and I spoke last time." Jackson's hand on my shoulder tensed for a moment. "Given Barbara's status as a low-level demon, and the fact that she never bound Robin's magic, breaking the pact is surprisingly straightforward."

"It is?" That shocked me. Had I lived this long under Barbara's thumb, getting weaker and feeling miserable, for no reason?

"It is. But, don't beat yourself up over that," Jessica said.

I nodded, unable to speak. If she was right, this would be over soon.

Evan and Matt came around from behind the half-circle table. "Jackson, help us move the chairs out of the way?" Evan asked.

"We need room for the ritual circle," Matt explained.

Jackson, Matt, and Evan moved the folding chairs to the edges of the room, clearing a large space. Theresa placed and lit four candles across from each other, as if at the edges of an unseen circle. Seeing my look, she chuckled.

"It's hard to draw a circle on the carpet. We learned that it's not always necessary." She shrugged and turned to confer with Jessica.

"We'll use the feminine strength of the Goddess for this ritual. So, men, we do not need you for this one. Could you stand behind the council table?" Jackson, Matt, and Evan obliged. "Marcie, please stand at due North. Theresa, due South. I'll go to East. And, Robin, you'll be West."

I waited until the other three had taken up their positions, since I wasn't sure which direction west would be, before assuming my own position.

"Is everybody ready?" Jessica asked.

We assented.

"At all times, remember our purpose in conducting this ritual. To break the pact between Robin and Barbara. First, we will call the corners. This will cleanse our space and help us open communication with the Goddess," Jessica said. She closed her brown eyes, took a deep breath.

I thought I would find the whole thing silly, but I found myself captivated by the process. It was as though something missing in my life for years was awakening.

"I call to the North, the element of Earth," Marcie began, her voice low and melodious.

"I call to the East, the element of Air," Jessica continued.

"I call to the South, the element of Fire," Theresa said.

I opened my mouth and nothing emerged. I swallowed past the lump in my throat, remembered my intention in calling the corners, and lifted my chin a fraction. "I call to the West, the element of Water."

Jessica nodded at me. "Robin, declare your intention. Use your name and be specific."

With a strong, clear voice, I spoke into the circle. "I, Robin Landon, desire to break my pact with Barbara Knollman." My hands fluttered. "Do we need her demon name?" I asked Jessica softly, but with audible panic in my voice. She shook her head.

Jessica pulled a vial of liquid from an unseen pocket of her loose green t-shirt dress. She opened the vial and sprinkled some into the center of the circle.

"I use this salt water for purification," she stated, clearly directing this explanation at me. She closed her eyes. I swore her red hair was glowing.

"We call upon the Goddess to hear Robin's plea, to break the pact with the demon, Barbara Knollman. We call upon Mother Earth to intervene to prevent the bond from reforming."

Wait. That could happen? My shoulders tensed and I gnawed at my lower lip.

"Farewell and blessed be," Jessica stated with a note of finality.

"Blessed be," the other ladies repeated. I think I caught on in time for at least the last two syllables. I assumed that would be sufficient.

The women lowered their heads in a moment of silence. I copied their mannerisms, and in my own moment of seriousness, sent my pure request into the world.

"Thank you, ladies," Jessica said with a bright smile around the circle.

Theresa walked the circle, blowing out and retrieving the candles. The men came forward to return the folding chairs to their prior positions.

It all seemed very anti-climactic. "And that'll work? To make the pact, I had to sign the bond in blood." I shuddered at the memory.

Jessica grinned. "Trust me, it worked."

My phone trilled an incoming call. Barbara. Blood drained from my face. "Hello?" I answered with a trembling voice.

"Hello, Robin. You've been busy."

I closed my eyes for a moment, gathering strength. "Yes, I have."

"I'd like to see you," she requested in a conversational tone.

"Why?"

"Old times' sake?"

I swore I heard a smile in her voice. Did she know something we didn't? "Sure. How about tomorrow morning?" I offered nonchalantly, but my pulse hammered in my head.

"See you then." She disconnected the call.

I turned to Jackson, the hand holding my cell phone shaking. He closed his strong fingers around mine.

"She can't hurt you," he said.

"You can't know that," I argued. "She'll kill me for breaking the pact. How did she even know I broke the pact?" I heard the hysterical note in my rising voice.

"She would have sensed an energy change," Jessica offered from across the room.

I nodded as I considered that. I made eye contact with Jackson. "Now what?"

"We need to talk," he said.

# CHAPTER TWENTY-THREE

Hurt shown in Jackson's eyes. The others had moved out of earshot to provide us privacy. He stood with his arms dangling at his sides. He seemed to be deciding how to open the conversation.

"So, you're a witch?"

"Yes."

"Interesting."

"Uh-huh."

"That might have been good information to have earlier." His voice had an edge to it.

"Probably."

"Could I get more than a one-word response, please?"

The exasperation in his voice was unsurprising and justified. "I missed my opportunity to tell you initially," I said. "Then it seemed too big a thing to mention until after all the issues were taken care of."

"That sounds like an excuse," he said in a tired voice.

"That's because it is," I admitted with a bark of unhappy laughter. "I didn't want to be judged for my poor choices."

"In signing a pact with a demon?"

"Um, yeah."

His eyes met mine and he gave a small shake of his head. "You didn't trust me."

"That's not exactly it," I floundered in my reply. "I didn't trust anybody and…" I swallowed. "I wanted you to like me." Good grief that sounded pathetic.

A real smile flitted across his face. "I did like you. I do like you," he amended. He reached out a hand to caress my neck. "I liked you from the beginning."

"Well, sure, your protection magic drew you to me." My heart hammered in my chest.

"That's true," he responded.

That's it? You've got nothing else? Frustration zinged through me. "At least now you don't have to protect me anymore," I said with feigned nonchalance.

"Mm-hmm," he agreed.

I picked at a cuticle then dropped my arms to my sides, mirroring him. "I should have been honest with you about it all," I blurted out.

"I could understand why you wouldn't want to go into details, but you kept some pretty big secrets from me. For no reason."

The confusion in his voice physically hurt. "I did."

"You were a witch. Believed your magic was bound. By a demon. With whom you signed a blood pact. Did I leave anything out?"

"I hurt people with my magic," I mumbled, as pain seared through me.

"Maybe."

"What do you mean, maybe? I killed my parents," I said in a hollow voice.

He collected his thoughts for a moment. "Your parents didn't understand what you were. Are. You therefore never received guidance for how to control your magic. Many things are set in stone; you don't know that your parents' fate wasn't already sealed," he said.

"That's a cop out, and you know it," I protested.

Jackson shrugged. "Maybe. Maybe not." He gave me a crooked smile. "Either way, you've paid penance. It's time to move forward."

With you? I wanted to ask the question, but I didn't. I simply nodded.

"I guess we'll be in touch?" His expression mixed hopeful longing with something shuttered that I couldn't read.

Ugh. More mixed signals. "I guess so."

With that apparently settled in his mind, Jackson turned and strode from the room. Jessica approached and took me by the elbow. She leaned in, almost conspiratorially. "Give him time."

"Why is that always what people recommend?"

She laughed. "Because people need time to process information that shocks their system."

I supposed she was right. Besides, I had a demon to meet with in – I checked my watch – eight hours. If I wanted to get some sleep so I could be bright-eyed and bushy-tailed in the morning, I needed to head for home. Oh, wait, Jackson drove me here.

"Would you mind giving me a lift home?"

"Not at all."

I wanted to be ready for my final scene with the demon. Hopefully, it wouldn't also be my curtain call.

*****

"Quit fidgeting," Barbara ordered. Her hands rested on the desk in front of her, talons clicking while she spoke.

I stilled my bouncing leg and twisting fingers, unaware I'd been doing either. "Sorry."

"You're apologizing?"

"You're right," I agreed. "Sorry." I rolled my eyes at myself.

Barbara stood from her desk and walked to the window overlooking Main Street. I stared at her sleek bun and red power suit. "You recovered your magic."

"I did." I allowed a bit of pride to seep into my voice. That was a mistake.

"You broke the pact," she said in a voice that froze the blood in my veins.

"We did."

She turned at that. "We?"

Quick internal debate on whether to disclose… "The Witches Council."

She nodded and retook her seat. "I didn't think you had the ability to break it on your own."

"I could have done that?"

She smiled her predatory smile, all sharp teeth and thinned lips. "Obviously not."

My face reddened at the insult to my magic. "Hey, I thought you bound my magic," I objected.

"You did think that. That was convenient for me, for you to think that," she said.

"Sneaky."

"I'm a demon."

"How did you know we broke the pact?"

She stared at me like I'd been dropped on my head too many times as a child. "I sensed the energy change between us."

Just like Jessica had guessed. "What happens now?" I asked and glanced down at the floor. Could she still suck me down to hell? Could she ever have done that?

Barbara sighed. "It's fine. As I predicted at our previous meeting, we've come to the end of our relationship."

I gulped.

"I'm. Not. Going. To. Kill. You," she said, enunciating each syllable.

"Thank Goddess," slipped out before I could stop the words.

Barbara rolled her eyes. "Little girl, you are no longer a concern of mine. Our pact is broken. The contract for the killing is null and void. I won't be pursuing that angle anymore. I've got some thinking to do on my next steps." She abruptly stopped, an expression of surprise on her face. Probably shocked she told me even that much.

Feeling emboldened by her uncertainty – and her declaration that she wasn't going to kill me – I stood tall and stared directly into her obsidian eyes. "I can't say this has been a positive experience. But it has been a learning one. Thank you for that, I suppose." I turned my back on her and took two steps toward the door.

"Are you sure you want to turn your back on me?" she asked in a silky voice and I froze. She laughed and I started moving again. "Good luck, little witch."

Her mocking laughter followed me out of the office and down the hall. At least it was over. I had plans that night to celebrate with my new friends. Should I invite Jackson? I knew I'd ponder the question all day.

# CHAPTER TWENTY-FOUR

"*Ciao*, Robin," Antonio's rich Italian voice greeted me when I entered the café that night. He air kissed my cheeks and then grasped my hands. His brown eyes met mine. "Welcome back to your family. For leaving the demon."

"Thank you, I haven't felt this good in years."

"*Prego, prego.* Please, join your friends. Anything you want tonight is on the house."

"*Grazi.*" Warmth suffused me as I walked through *Soprannaturale.* Nobody avoided my gaze, glared at me behind hooded lids, or frowned when they saw me. I hastened my steps at the sight of Catherine, Alex, Evie, Ryan, Mia, and Jacob sitting around the back booth. I wasn't surprised Liz wasn't there. Those fences hadn't been mended yet, I guessed.

My heart stuttered at the lack of Jackson. I never did call to invite him, though.

"Robin!" Catherine pushed the others over to make room for me.

"I can pull up a chair," I said uncertainly. Seven around the booth seemed tight.

"Not at all," Mia responded. "Have a seat."

I slid in beside Catherine. Ryan handed me a menu. I perused it while the group's chatter resumed.

"What do you think she'll do next?" Evie asked.

"I don't know," Catherine answered. "From the moment I arrived in town, she's acted like we have a connection and I'm somehow important to her goals." She shrugged. "But, since I helped thwart her this time, I imagine she feels differently now." Laughter erupted at the sentiment.

"What do you think, Robin?" Evie asked. I set the menu down. "You worked with her for years. Did she ever give any hint of her end game?"

I shook my head. "No, she didn't. Catherine's right, though. She became Barbara's focus from the moment she arrived; and then by extension, everyone connected with the Paranormal Talent Agency."

"So strange," Alex said.

"I know. She dropped cryptic hints all the time," I said, "but never anything substantial. But I don't care anymore," I declared. "She's out of my life."

"Here, here," the group chanted, everyone lifting their water in unison.

"To Robin living her full life again," Mia toasted.

"To Robin," they repeated.

"Yeah, I have to say," Evie chimed in. "You looked washed out before. You look so much better now."

"Evie!" Mia chastised her.

"No, it's okay," I assured them. "I understand. I didn't realize it was happening at the time, but being tethered to the demon was sucking out my life force." That statement piqued Alex's interest. "Not quite the way an incubus does, Alex," I explained. "Just a slow steady drain. Fatigue. Lack of joy. But I didn't really notice, believe it or not. I thought I was sad because I'd decided to work with a demon."

"Choices have consequences," Evie quipped.

I nodded. "I know. I just never made the connection. I became paranoid. Didn't want to be around anyone. Didn't want anybody in my life. It became all about Barbara. Until I met—" I bit off Jackson's name. "—all of you. Thanks."

"You're welcome," Catherine responded. "It's great to see how your eyes sparkle and your skin glows now."

"I feel like I've rediscovered who I am, even apart from simply not being a demon's minion."

Catherine tilted her head. Dang, I'd bet her magical abilities identified that as an incomplete truth. But I didn't want to talk about Jackson. Tonight's dinner was focused on celebrating our victories.

I lifted my water again. "To reaching Day 7 of Barbara's Killer Countdown with nobody being killed."

"To reaching Day 7," they repeated, spilling water with their vigorous bumping of glasses.

"To Robin getting her magic back," Catherine toasted.

"To Robin breaking the contract with the demon," Mia added.

"And to you guys. Without your help—" I set my glass down, swallowed past the lump in my throat, ignored the burning tears in my eyes. "Without your help, none of this would have been possible. I can never thank you enough."

Catherine hugged me tightly. "Don't give up on him," she whispered. She didn't explain her comment. Of course, I knew who she meant.

Jackson.

I pulled out my phone and texted him.

*Sorry for the last minute invite. Wanna swing by the café on Main Street to celebrate with us?*

I placed the cellphone on the vinyl beside me. "What's next for you guys?" I asked the group. I half-listened to their answers, waiting for the vibration of Jackson's reply.

There!

"Excuse me," I told them before picking up the phone. They exchanged knowing glances. My super-secret spy skills were clearly subpar.

*Working another hour or so. After?*

*How about my place?*

*It's a date.*

It was a date?

## CHAPTER TWENTY-FIVE

An hour later I didn't move when the doorbell rang. I knew it was Jackson, since I invited him, but I didn't know what I was going to say. So, of course, I went with awkward.

"You're here."

"Like an unexpected sequel." He leaned toward me, hands braced on either side of the doorway. "May I come in?"

I pretended to consider his request. "Sequels are usually disappointing."

He gripped his chest in mock pain. "What about *The Godfather Part II*?"

"Ooh, a classic." We grinned at each other. I moved from the doorway. "In that case, come on in. Besides, I invited you, didn't I?"

Jackson gave an exaggerated bow and stepped through my doorway. I giggled at the theatrics. A meow stopped me from closing the door. I peered past Jackson into the dark and my eyes widened when a flash of fur ran by me into the house.

"Hey!" I turned to follow the animal, but it hadn't gone far, sitting only a few feet inside the door.

"Did you adopt a cat?" Jackson asked.

"No," I answered, but my eyes were glued to the cat sitting before me, whiskers twitching. "Patches," I whispered. "It can't be."

"Patches? Wasn't that your cat who—"

"Ran off almost ten years ago," I said. "How is this possible?"

My mind flooded with images from my life, from the moment of the accident to this moment right now. I watched the cat; she almost seemed to be nodding. Could she be seeing these images too?

"She's your familiar," Jackson said into my ear.

"My what? Oh, my."

"Meow," the cat said again.

I crouched down and the cat padded over. We head-butted, unshed tears blurring my vision. "Are you my familiar?"

"Meow."

New images flooded my mind, and they seemed to be coming from… the cat. I watched the last ten years of her life flash by like a movie in my mind. When it finished, I rose and faced Jackson.

"And?"

I chuckled. "After the accident and I disavowed my abilities, she was... temporarily reassigned, I guess. To another teenaged witch who needed a familiar." I bit my lower lip and met Jackson's eyes. "This other witch was fated to die," I said. "And then Patches came back to me when I'd rediscovered my abilities."

"Wow."

"That's an understatement," I agreed. "Welcome home, Patches." At her name, my little black, white, and orange furball strolled to the couch, stretched out her front legs, and then jumped up. She settled herself in and began bathing. With a shake of my head, I turned back to Jackson.

"I'm going to need a minute to adjust to that." I stepped toward the kitchen. "Do you want something to drink?"

"Sure, I'll take a glass of red wine. Whatever you have is fine."

"Long day of filming?" I asked from the kitchen.

"Not too bad."

I handed him a wineglass and sat beside him on the loveseat. Patches' quiet purring created background noise. Jackson and I simultaneously sipped our wine. Was he nervous, too?

"How have you been?"

"Since yesterday?" I asked with a grin.

"Your life is full of adventure."

My smile slipped. "Yeah, a little too much."

Jackson set his wineglass on the coffee table. "I sense this is a more serious meeting than I thought from your text."

I traced the edge of my wineglass with my finger before setting it down next to his. "I like you. I liked you from the first moment I saw you." I held up a hand to stop him from interrupting. "It started out as attraction—" I flushed at his wolfish grin. "—but then you stepped up, supporting me, helping me reclaim my life. Plus, you're smart, funny…" I shook my head and his grin faded. "But I don't know if it's real."

He gave me his inscrutable look that I'd already come to recognize as his deep-thinking face. "Why would you doubt if it's real?"

I waved my hand dismissively. "I thought there was something there… until you explained about your protection magic drawing you to me. I'm telling you this because I'm trying to start my reclaimed life on the right foot. With total honesty. I don't want you to feel obligated to—" He put his finger up to my lips.

In shock, I stopped talking. Was he shushing me? Was I making him that uncomfortable? Although, the gleam in his eye confused me. This whole honesty thing was a challenge!

Jackson took my hands in his, rubbing his thumbs along the pads of my palms. "Robin. You're correct that my protection magic drew me to you. But it was never just about protection. I was attracted to you from the first moment I saw you, too."

"Even with the demon energy diminishing me?" I couldn't help but ask.

He chuckled. "I'll admit, I wondered if you had recently been ill, the first time I saw you. Even still, there was a spark."

"My magic?"

He lifted a single shoulder in a shrug. "Maybe. I don't know. That spark drew me in. And yes, my magic told me you needed protecting. Then…" He paused and leaned in closer, his breath warm against my cheek. "These past few days I saw the real you, hidden beneath the demon influence and self-doubt."

"In only a few days?"

"Didn't you just say you felt the same way after a few days?"

"Your logic is infallible," I agreed, voice husky and breathy.

"Thank you. I am drawn to you in every way that a man can be to a woman. Protection magic or not."

"Me too," I whispered. I felt the now-familiar tingle as magic raced along my arms to my fingers. Tiny sparks showered us as we embraced and I ran my hand over his buzz cut hair. Jackson pulled back and the sparks extinguished. His eyes were wide.

"Where are you getting the energy? Is a storm coming?"

"Oh yes, there is," I purred and leaned into him again. His lips met mine, gentle pressure sending non-magical energy through my body. His arms tightened around me and we enjoyed the moment. We separated with a sigh.

"I discovered I could pull energy from just a simple household outlet," I informed him with a Cheshire-cat grin. He laughed low and sexy and we embraced again, enjoying our happily-for-right-now that just might become our happily-ever-after.

# EPILOGUE

"Robin Landon, fancy meeting you here." The iron voice brought me to a dead stop, and I turned to find myself staring into Barbara's unblinking obsidian eyes.

"Hi, Barbara," I stammered out. "Not too surprising, since we're both members of the Chamber."

She lifted an eyebrow at my tone. "I see you've also found your backbone."

I reflexively stood up straighter and Barbara chuckled. "Yes, I have," I said in a low, but clear voice. I might have found my backbone since breaking the pact; I still didn't want to make unnecessary waves by drawing attention.

"I'm glad," Barbara said.

"You are?"

She shrugged. "I don't hold a grudge."

I belly laughed and then clapped hands over my mouth. "Maybe not, but you ordered Jackson's death. You ordered my death!" Her eyes bored into my skull at my exhalation and I waited to be pulled down to Hell, before remembering she said all was forgiven. Maybe she didn't hold grudges? Demons were confusing when they didn't stay heartless and deadly.

"That might have been a mistake," she said.

"What?" I surely misheard that.

"That might have been a mistake, ordering your deaths," she repeated and expanded.

"You're a demon. A killer," I insisted.

"I've never actually killed anyone," Barbara said archly. "Directly or indirectly."

"Now why do I find that hard to believe?"

"Because you don't like me." Her smile revealed rows of tiny, sharp teeth. "Because you were my minion for years."

"That's true." I hesitated. Oh, why not? "What will you do now?"

Barbara's eyebrows rose in surprise. "Why do you care?"

I shrugged. "Natural curiosity, I suppose."

She opened and closed her mouth. "I don't know," she admitted. "Everything had been going according to plan, as I saw in my premonitions. But, this series of events was unseen. And I don't know what that means." She bit her lower lip, a strangely human action that threw me for a moment.

"I hope you figure it out. Maybe you don't have to let your—" I coughed. "—demon status determine your actions."

Barbara chuckled. "You mean, I can choose to be good."

Despite her sarcastic response, I thought I heard an undercurrent of genuine uncertainty. "Yes. You can choose a different path." Did demons have free will like that? I had no idea.

Barbara's eyes flashed red for a moment and the blood chilled in my veins. Had I gone too far? They returned to their normal obsidian, and I breathed a sigh of relief into the uncomfortable silence.

"Maybe I will." Barbara sighed. "Maybe I will."

Read the continuing story of Barbara Knollman, repentant demon, in Episode Five of the Paranormal Talent Agency!

# THANK YOU!

Thank you so much for supporting my work and reading this book. I truly hope you enjoyed reading it as much as I did writing it.

**If you liked the book, please consider leaving a review online.**

Just a few lines would be great. Reviews are not only the highest compliment you can pay to an author, they also help other readers discover and make more informed choices about purchasing books in a crowded online space. Thank you so much in advance.

If you didn't like the book or have concerns, please email me directly at
heather@heathersilvio.com

# ABOUT THE AUTHOR

Heather has written fiction and nonfiction; she is also an actress and licensed psychologist. When she isn't working, she channels her inner flapper as a 1920s jazz and blues singer.

Visit http://www.heathersilvio.com for more information and to sign up for her New Releases and Appearances Newsletter.

www.ingramcontent.com/pod-product-compliance
Lightning Source LLC
Chambersburg PA
CBHW030207130726
47898CB00012B/908